PUFFIN BOOKS

The Bully

...lle was born on the south coast of England in
...d moved to the North-West twenty years later.
... ...ritten more than twenty books for children, as
... ...novels and television drama for adults and chil-
... ...e also writes for stage and radio. He lives in
... ...m, Lancashire.

Also by Jan Needle

THE THIEF

For Younger Readers
THE WAR OF THE WORMS

The Bully

Jan Needle

PUFFIN BOOKS

PUFFIN BOOKS

Published by the Penguin Group
Penguin Books Ltd, 27 Wrights Lane, London W8 5TZ, England
Penguin Books USA Inc., 375 Hudson Street, New York, New York, 10014, USA
Penguin Books Australia Ltd, Ringwood, Victoria, Australia
Penguin Books Canada Ltd, 10 Alcorn Avenue, Toronto, Ontario, Canada M4V 3B2
Penguin Books (NZ) Ltd, 182–190 Wairau Road, Auckland 10, New Zealand

Penguin Books Ltd, Registered Offices: Harmondsworth, Middlesex, England

First published by Hamish Hamilton 1993
Published in Puffin Books 1995
3 5 7 9 10 8 6 4

Copyright © Jan Needle, 1993
All rights reserved

The moral right of the author has been asserted

Filmset in Monophoto Times

Printed in England by Clays Ltd, St Ives plc

In memory of
Richard Thomas Hargreaves Rosthorn

CHAPTER ONE

It was a game to the children, just a game. Their headteacher, Mrs Beryl Stacey, saw danger everywhere, in the abandoned chalkpits where the rock could crumble and throw you to your death, in the marshes by the sea-shore where the bad men lurked, in the high-speed roads that took the traffic racing by the school. Mrs Beryl Stacey could see danger even on the playing fields, and issued lots of warnings every term. To the children, it was all a game.

Today, the game was stalking. From the moment he had woken up, Simon Mason had decided to go on the offensive, to take the war into the enemy camp. He would leave home early – which would surprise his mother – he would detect his targets, and he would keep them under observation. For once, he would not forget his football kit, because he would need his towel to hide a weapon in. *That* would surprise Mr Kershaw.

Simon's room was very small, and very cluttered. He wore pyjama tops and a pair of underpants, and to dress merely put on his black school trousers, pulled off the top, and hauled on a grey shirt over his yellow tee-shirt. His football kit was where he'd dropped it last week, complete with towel. No, not last week, last week he'd forgotten and been told off. Simon picked up the roll and sniffed the towel. Manky.

'Simon!'

His mother's voice was thin, piercing up the stairwell from the kitchen. The TV was on, a thicker, deeper note. He shouted back triumphantly: 'I'm up, I'm up! Okay!?'

The room was full of weapons, feet deep in them. There was a machine-gun that looked almost real in half-light, and a huge revolver that would have gone down a treat with Arnie Schwarzenegger, except that its barrel was bent. But there was the martial arts thing that was real, the killer keyring. Simon picked it up, black and polished, and felt the weight of it. Yes, it was genuine, okay, his Uncle George had got it for him for his birthday. You could give someone a nasty poke with it, for sure, but he supposed there must be more to it than that, he supposed it was a killer weapon, somehow. Uncle George had promised to find out.

For the moment, though, it would do to give a nasty poke. Unbidden, Simon saw a face before his eyes, a girl's face with blonde hair. Unbidden, his teeth clamped shut, ground against each other. She was the target.

'Simon! Come *on*, love, you'll be late. I know you're not up yet, you'll miss your breakfast.'

Simon laughed, and rolled the keyring into the towel. He felt the grubby bundle, felt the football shoes he hated. He hated all of school, but games he hated worst. All the kids running about like idiots trying to *win* things, and Mr Kershaw with his whistle, egging them on. Perhaps he'd get him one day, too, when he knew exactly how the keyring worked.

It was a daft thought, but a pleasing one, which kept Simon happy down the first long road out of the estate. It was an odd estate, divided up between two schools, and none of the other kids in his street went to St Michael's, not that there were many of them anyway. Those that did live nearby went down the hill to school, while Simon had to walk along the side of it, and round the curve, and into the 'better' part of town, as his mother sometimes called it. Once he was out of the tacky, scruffy streets and in among the trees and big green gardens, Simon would see uniforms like his, although in rather smarter nick. Usually inside a car, also. The sort of car that he could only dream of driving in.

But first – before the tree-lined streets – Simon had to pass the chalkpit. It was derelict, a white gash in the hillside, reached by a dusty access track that had no houses on it, only piles of rubbish and an abandoned car. He stopped and stared towards the rusty iron gates, at the tumble-down buildings and the junk. Behind it all rose the chalk face, a crumbling cliff criss-crossed with little pathways, bored with shafts and tunnels.

3

Simon felt the pull of it, he often went to play and hide there, away from kids and grown-ups, football games and school. He loved the place. It was peace and comfort. It was solitude.

Trouble, too. He told himself he could track his prey from one of the high ledges – but he knew he lied. From up there he could see the town laid out beneath him, and the glittering sea, but not the streets close by, which were masked by houses. Today was stalking day, stalking Anna Royle and her brother and their friend Rebekkah. If he went up to the chalkpit he would miss them, and he would be in trouble if someone spotted him. Mrs Stacey was very hot on places like the chalkpit. They were *dangerous*.

The games teacher – Mr Brian Kershaw – was watching when Simon reached St Michael's playing fields, and he knew immediately that something was going on. Simon was walking like an extra in a spy film, keeping close into a wall, and at one point he stooped and seemed to pick up something from the turf. Mr Kershaw, to amuse himself, put his whistle to his lips and blew a short, sharp blast. All around him children stopped and looked, but Simon did not hear. Mr Kershaw dropped his whistle and let it dangle on its ribbon. Time to get started with the teams. Time enough to sort out Simon Mason later.

Across the broad expanse of muddy grass, he saw Louise Shaw. Although she was deputy headteacher, it was general games this morning, and she was helping with the smaller kids. As she got nearer, Brian squared his shoulders in his stark blue tracksuit and waved.

'That's a lot of whistle you've got there,' she said, amiably. 'Don't wear it out before games start, will you?'

Mr Kershaw nodded towards the old pavilion.

'One of the bad boys,' he said. 'He's gone behind there, like Jack the Ripper. I was trying to head off a disaster.'

Miss Shaw turned to look. There were several knots of children by the building now. One group she recognised.

'Surely not David Royle?' She laughed lightly. 'His mother wouldn't like to hear him called a bad boy. He's got the lovely Anna with him, anyway, and Rebekkah Tanner. Hardly the Mafia, Brian!'

The children disappeared behind the building. 'I meant Simon Mason,' Brian Kershaw said. 'The Lump. He's round there waiting for them.'

A faint look of disapproval moved across Louise Shaw's face.

'Brian,' she said. 'Don't call him names.'

'Sorry,' he replied. 'It's not as if there's anybody listening, though. You know he's trouble. He's a nuisance. I think he picked a rock up on his way.'

'You think. But you don't know.'

'Look,' said Mr Kershaw, 'however bad I am at putting things, I think we ought to check. Do you want me to go, or will you? I've got three games to start, if your lot aren't ready yet.'

Indeed, there was a clump of children pressing in towards them, a sea of pink knees and faces. Louise nodded.

'I'll go,' she said. 'It's probably nothing, anyway.'

Anna Royle was a tall girl for her age. Tall, and confident and very nice. Rebekkah Tanner was her best friend and her neighbour, and their two houses were rather isolated from everybody else's. Because of this, perhaps, they were very close.

They had talked about the Simon Mason problem as they were driven into school by Anna's mother, and Anna and Rebekkah had discussed it on the phone quite late the night before. David, who had gone to bed earlier than his sister, being younger, wanted to know what they had decided. As usual, he had opened his mouth too wide and put his foot in it.

'What was that, David?' asked their mother, from the front. 'Did you say bullying?'

Anna glared at him. Even the back of the Volvo estate was not vast enough for them to talk in private.

'Not exactly bullying, Mrs Royle,' put in Rebekkah politely. 'It's just the games this morning. Sometimes some of the boys get rough, that's all.'

'It's more enthusiasm than anything,' added Anna, smiling at her friend. 'You know how David exaggerates, the little squirt.'

Mrs Royle glanced backwards. She had a strong face like her daughter's, although not quite so attractive.

6

'Don't you listen to them, David, you're not a little squirt at all.' She paused. 'You would tell me, though, wouldn't you? If there was really any nastiness like that?'

The children made faces at each other. She was worrying about the school again. *Her* mother, their gran, had always disapproved about them going to a State school. They were the first ones in the family who ever had.

'Oh, Mum,' said Anna. 'Don't start that again. It's a *good* school, St Michael's, we have a great time there.'

'And anyway,' said Rebekkah, 'we've got David, haven't we? He's a match for *any* rough boy!'

The woman and the girls joined in the laughter, while David stared stolidly through the window at the crowds of children heading for the gate. Sometimes he felt ganged up on.

'Ah well,' said Mrs Royle, as the doors were opened and they piled on to the pavement. 'I suppose you're right. There seem so *many* of them, though. Are you *quite* sure that . . .'

But her children, and Rebekkah, were hurtling round the throng, school-bags and games kit flying out behind them.

Certainly, she told herself, they seemed happy enough. She put the Volvo into gear and nosed it gently through the crowds of milling children.

Some of them looked so very *rough*, she thought.

*

Mr Kershaw had been right about the rock –
Simon had seen a juicy one and picked it up, in
case it came in useful for the ambush. He had
seen the Volvo pull up by the kerb and had
ducked behind the old pavilion with a sudden
mix of fear and excitement in his stomach. He
had the rock, he had the keyring. Maybe they
hadn't seen him, though.

They had, and retribution was extremely swift.
Simon had tripped over his foot in getting to the
place, and dropped his towel, scattering the kit.
He was on one knee when Anna burst around the
corner.

'He's armed!' she shouted, jubilantly. 'The little
spassie's armed!'

Simon's fantasies of warfare and revenge lay in
the mud, scattered like his dirty football gear. He
got clumsily to his feet as David joined Anna, his
stomach going hollow. Rebekkah's tousled head
appeared, then she took station at the corner to
keep a watch-out.

'Simon, Simon, little Simple Simon!' chanted
David. 'Spastic, spastic, spastic!'

Simon let the hand that held the rock drop to
his side. To Anna it was obvious what he was
hoping for.

'You can't fool me!' she shouted. 'I can see the
stone! You were going to throw it at me, weren't
you? You're a bully, aren't you?'

As she darted in to hit him she was laughing.
Simon's face – rather round and hopeless –
twisted in his fear. But he was trying, also, to

form a smile. A supplicating smile, a pleading smile, ingratiating.

'Yerk!' went Anna Royle, in mock disgust. 'You're a creep as well!'

She danced up to him and punched him in the face, feeling his nose bend squashily beneath her knuckles. As she drew her hand away, his face crumpled satisfyingly. There would be tears.

'Look out!' Rebekkah hissed. 'Miss is coming! Miss Shaw!'

She sounded frightened. She'd left it too late, she'd forgotten to look out because she'd wanted to watch the fun.

'Simple Simon!' chanted David, and Rebekkah squeaked to interrupt him.

'Shut *up*! Shut *up*!' It was a cross between a whisper and a cry. Two seconds later Louise Shaw strode purposefully into sight.

But not before Anna had dropped her school bag and her rolled towel to the ground and spread it with a kick. Not before she had dropped to one knee and put a look of anguish on her face.

'Oh, Miss,' she cried, 'he hit me, Miss, he hit me!'

To the children, it was just a game . . .

CHAPTER TWO

Miss Shaw, for a split second, was reminded of a Christmas tableau. Simon stood gazing at her awkwardly, his round face confused and sad. Anna knelt before him on one knee, her head turned across her shoulder at Louise, her long blonde hair sprayed across her cheek. David, small and startled, seemed poised between fear and flight, while Rebekkah wore an anxious, humble smile – the Wise Man who had brought the cheapest, useless gift. Then the tableau came to life.

'Miss!' said Rebekkah, 'I saw him hit her, Miss! I think he's hurt her, Miss!'

Anna immediately looked more hurt. She tried to get up off her knee, but gave a little catch of pain. Rebekkah ran to help.

David was pointing dramatically at Simon.

'He's got a rock, Miss! There! He could've killed her, Miss!'

Simon had a rock. A jagged, flinty thing, big as a cooking apple. Miss Shaw noticed that he was standing on his football shorts, adding fresh mud to the dried. She wondered why his mother had not washed the old mud off.

'I've hurt my leg, Miss,' Anna moaned. 'He kicked me, Miss. I think I might be badly injured.'

Miss Shaw moved briskly, aware that things could get out of hand if not controlled. Anna, surprised, found herself being jerked none too gently to her feet.

'Nonsense, Anna. Don't over-dramatise. Now, run along and change, please. Mr Kershaw and Mrs Hendry will be picking teams.'

'But Miss . . .'

Louise checked her over with a practised eye. There was mud on her knee, above the long white sock. Nothing more. David, an obedient and helpful boy, was picking up his sister's kit.

'No buts. If you still feel bad after you've changed we'll go along to the office and lie you down for an hour or two, to see if anything develops. Even playing netball would be preferable to that, surely?'

Ruefully, Anna gave in. She did not smile, however. She was not going to let the teacher win so easily, nor Simple Simon Mason.

'But what about him?' She tossed her head. 'Aren't you going to punish him? It's not the first time, Miss.'

Simon had not moved. He stood awkwardly, a little fat, ill-dressed and somehow useless. The Lump, Brian had called him. Louise felt a mix of sympathy and irritation. He was trouble, certainly, he was always trouble. But he was pathetic, somehow, too.

11

'Never you mind,' she told Anna. 'I'll sort it out and I'll do the necessary. Pick up your school-bag, please, and run along. Honestly, two great strapping girls intimidated by one boy, I don't know!'

Anna said coldly: 'I hope you're not suggesting we should fight back, Miss Shaw? I don't know what my father would say to that. It's against the school rules, too.'

Louise watched them go after that exchange. When she turned back to Simon he had moved slightly. He had dropped the rock to hide it, and it had landed on his football shirt.

'Well, Simon? And what have you got to say about all this?'

Inside his head, there was plenty that he might have said. But instead of saying it, instead of raising his eyes to the teacher's and trying to get it out, Simon took the easy way. His head went lower, his shoulders rounded, he shuffled slightly. Even recognising that the movements were defensive, Miss Shaw was irritated.

'Look, love, I haven't got all day, you know. Who started it?'

He remembered waking up, his dreams of vengeance, of smashing Anna Royle's face. He would have started it, if he'd dared.

'Look,' went on Miss Shaw, her voice considerably thinner. 'I'm not going to label you a bully just on Anna's say-so, if that's what you think. But you must tell me what happened. You must answer my questions. Simon! Tell me!'

Behind her, she could hear the babble of children getting organised into teams. She heard a whistle that she recognised as Carol Hendry's, shrill and impatient. Carol Hendry would be impatient with *her* if she did not appear soon to do her bit.

'Simon,' she said. 'As I came up just now, I heard some words. I heard "Simple Simon", I heard "spastic". Were they addressed to you?'

She realised suddenly that he was not quite right, this boy. Standing before her with his head bent forward, he still managed to look clumsy, as if he might fall over. He did fall over quite a lot, in fact, he was quite famous for it. He was slow at reading, too. And writing, and arithmetic. It came to her, standing there, that no one could have called him lucky.

When she spoke again, her voice had softened.

'Does this happen very often, this sort of thing?' she asked. 'Do people pick on you a lot?'

They were interrupted by the impatient Mrs Hendry. She came around the corner of the pavilion all arms and legs and bustle.

'Oh, sorry, Louise. Brian told me you were . . . Look, sorry to interfere but we could do with some back-up on the field of battle.'

Louise bit her lip.

'Yes, okay,' she said, reluctantly. 'I'll be with you in a second.'

Mrs Hendry had already gone. Simon was looking at her face, as if he had already spoken.

'I'm sorry?' said Louise, in case he had. 'Did you answer me?'

13

He shook his head, then dropped his chin on to his chest again.

'Well, I mean to get to the bottom of it,' the teacher said, briskly. 'If there's bullying going on I'm going to put a stop to it. But how can I help you if you won't answer me?'

You can't help me anyway, thought Simon. No one can, can they? Not if Anna Royle has a say as well. He mumbled something, something meant to sound reassuring. Not real words.

'Come again?' said Miss Shaw. 'It's no use muttering.'

'It doesn't matter, Miss,' he said. 'It doesn't matter.'

'Hhm,' went Louise.

CHAPTER THREE

David, on instructions from his sister and her friend, went up to Simon in the changing room after games to ask him what Miss Shaw had said to him. David was afraid of Simon, but standing only in his underpants he did not appear too frightening.

'Anna says to tell you,' said David, boldly, 'that if you drop us in it there'll be mega-trouble, right? What happened?'

Simon did his best to ignore him. David was already dressed, his hair still wet and shiny from the shower. Simon had gone to the showers late, and found the water cold. He had rubbed the worst of the mud off with his towel.

'You,' said David. He was wearing shoes, and Simon was almost naked, so he felt pretty safe. 'What did she say? Old Loo-roll?'

'Nothing,' replied Simon. He pulled his shirt up over his head, disappeared into it, tried to hide.

'You didn't say it was us, did you? You didn't tell her any lies?'

'I didn't tell her nothing,' replied the emerging head. 'Leave me alone.'

The crowd in the changing room was thinning. Another lesson, soon.

'You'd better not have done,' David ended, lamely. 'Anna said to tell you. If there's any comeback, it's the worse for you, okay? Okay?'

Over David's shoulder, Simon saw Mr Kershaw bearing down on them. He began to jerk frantically at his trousers, trying to get them up his legs.

'You!' snapped the games master. 'Why aren't you dressed yet? Your hair's dry. Have you had your shower?'

A smile came over David's polished face as he walked away. It broadened as Mr Kershaw began to bellow.

'Filthy! Your chest is filthy, your legs are filthy, your clothes are filthy! Give me that towel, boy!'

David heard a clattering noise, then a silence. The few other boys left in the changing room had gone as still as mice, in case it should be their turn next. The note of Mr Kershaw's voice had changed.

'What's this, then? It came out of your towel. What is it, boy?'

David stopped, curious. Turning his head, he saw Mr Kershaw's brilliant blue bottom sticking out from underneath a bench. Simon, beside the teacher, looked cold and anxious, clutching his towel to his chest.

'It's a kubutan, isn't it?' The games master was standing up, holding something that looked like a small black rod with a silver ring attached. 'It's a dangerous weapon, isn't it?'

All eyes were fixed on him, and in an instant he became aware of it. He lifted back his head and roared.

'You lot! Finish up and out of here! All of you! Or you'll all be in for half an hour after school!'

They began to scurry, with David taking up the lead. A dangerous weapon! Simon Mason had a dangerous weapon! Wait till Anna and Rebekkah got to hear of this!

Simon, meanwhile, was answering Mr Kershaw's question. As honestly as he could.

'Please sir, I don't know,' he said.

The news that Simon was in some extra trouble was a balm to Anna and Rebekkah, although the 'deadly weapon' aspect did not impress them much.

'What was it, exactly?' Rebekkah asked. 'It sounds mad to me.'

David was not sure.

'Kershaw had it hidden in his hand,' he said. 'He didn't want us all to know. But he was furious, there's trouble brewing, honestly, big trouble.'

The three of them were in the playground. It was break. Although Anna would not have admitted it, they were skulking, keeping out of sight. They did not want to be observed by any of the teachers, Miss Shaw least of all.

'Oh well,' she said. 'If Kershaw was giving him

a rollicking, he can't have told on us, can he? That's one thing.'

'He called it something,' said David, suddenly. 'A Rubik's cube or something. A cubee-something.'

'You're a fool,' Rebekkah snorted. She was smiling, though, she was not unfriendly. 'A Rubik's cube, I ask you!'

Anna's face had clouded. She'd had a serious thought.

'Whatever it was,' she said, 'it means that Simon Mason had a weapon, so we're in the clear. He was going to attack us and we had to fight back. It was self-defence.'

'He had a rock, as well,' Rebekkah pointed out. 'Even old Loo-roll Louise saw that.'

They started to move slowly across the tarmac of the playground. David's face was scared.

'But they couldn't blame us anyway, could they?' he said. 'Not over Spassie Mason?'

It came to Anna that her brother must be right. No one would disbelieve them on the say-so of a nasty, dirty boy like that. She felt a stab of anger at him.

'He's a nuisance,' she said. 'He's a rotten nuisance. Maybe we should complain about the deadly weapon. He'd have hurt us if he could have done. He could have hurt us badly.'

'With his exploding Rubik's cube,' Rebekkah said, almost mockingly. Anna grinned.

'Don't knock it, kid,' she said, in a TV American accent. 'Even Loo-roll couldn't back up a boy who carries weapons, could she?'

David, mooching to a lesson on his own, was comforted.

Louise, in fact, merely found the weapon story irritating.

Mr Kershaw told her about it – with an air of mystery and of triumph – as they walked back into school together at the end of the lunch break.

'It was wrapped up in his kit,' he said. 'Amazing, really, that such a young kid should be carrying one. It's a martial arts thing.'

'What did you call it? A cubiton? What does it do, exactly?'

'Kubutan,' said Brian. 'With a K. In the right hands it can knock you unconscious, so I'm told. Pressure points or something. I'm not into martial arts, I couldn't tell you precisely how it works.'

'Could Simon Mason?'

He was amused.

'I wouldn't think so for a moment. It actually looks like a keyring, although he didn't have a key on it.'

'So it's hardly an offensive weapon, is it?' She was exasperated. 'Really, Brian, aren't you making a mountain out of a molehill over this? You didn't even confiscate it, did you?'

A faint flush came to his freckled face.

'I gave him a good verballing. I pinned his ears back. I thought that would be enough.'

'I'm sure it was,' said Louise, dryly. 'Your shouts are famous, Brian.'

They walked in silence for a while. The trouble

was, for Mr Kershaw, that she made him, often, feel a bit uncouth.

'So how are you planning to punish him?' he said, finally. 'For the bullying? He needs a short, sharp shock, that boy. He could grow up into a thug.'

They were walking down the last stretch to the school. It was quiet, almost rural, with a few children scattered about, clean and peaceful in their uniforms. Hardly the sort of place for breeding thugs, she thought.

'Oh, I don't know.' She sighed. 'The trouble is, I'm not convinced that he's the one to blame. I can't quite see him as a raging bully.'

'But he had a lump of rock to chuck at them. He even had a kubutan, as it turns out.'

'I know. And the lovely Anna Royle said he knocked her down, and kicked her. The trouble is, I'm not sure of the truth.'

They were almost at the school gates. Mr Kershaw stopped, looking at her curiously. She stopped with him.

'The lovely Anna,' he quoted. 'Don't you like her?'

She shrugged.

'Doesn't everybody? It doesn't mean I have to believe every word she utters, does it? I've got a nagging doubt, that's all.'

'Without a shred of evidence. While on the other hand . . .'

Louise laughed at him. She headed briskly through the gates into the yard.

'Even if Simon is a bully,' she said, 'I'm giving him the benefit of the doubt. There wasn't any harm done, whoever's fault it was this morning. I'm going to see if he'll respond to kindness. A surprise.'

'Meaning?'

'You'll have to wait and see,' she said.

CHAPTER FOUR

The real surprise, it turned out, was the way the kids reacted to her plan. The apologetic smile she wore to interrupt Mrs Earnshaw's lesson was wiped off within seconds.

'Sorry to intrude,' she said – although the lesson was all but over – 'but I want to appoint the next pets' monitor.'

The children got quite keen and noisy, because it was a position everybody coveted. It was a treat, a privilege, that was awarded now and then if somebody had been mega-good, or come out of hospital, or was new and lonely in the school. There had not been a monitor for several weeks.

'Now settle down,' she went on. 'I'm not here to choose somebody, I've already done that, I'm just here to tell. Simon, stand up, please. I want you to—'

But she was shouted down, her voice was drowned completely. As Simon stood, the others also clattered to their feet, yelling furiously.

'Simon *Mason*?! What, *him*?! Miss, Miss! You must be *joking*! But he's an *idiot*, Miss!'

Those were the words she could pick out. But

22

it was mostly just noise, a violent flow of anger from the thirty or so throats. Miss Shaw was horrified.

Mrs Earnshaw, an older, stricter woman, was banging on her table-top with a book. She was red with anger.

'Stop it! That's enough! You! Richard Harvey! Tanya! Sit down at once!'

The noise subsided and the class – including Simon – sat. Louise stepped forward firmly. She cleared her throat.

'Well,' she said. 'What was that about, I wonder. Will anybody tell me? Will anybody tell me to my face if they object to anything I've said?'

The children were embarrassed. They all liked Miss Shaw, and they were ashamed. Simon was slumped, staring at the surface of the table he was sharing with three other boys. He looked so unhappy that for a moment she was afraid. Perhaps it would be cruel to single him out. Perhaps he'd be happier to be left invisible in the crowd.

But she had started. She had better finish, and she knew it.

'I have to say,' she said, 'that your outburst quite disgusted me. You had not even got the self-control to let me finish, you don't even know what I was going to say.'

Richard Harvey, in the front row, shot up his hand and opened eager lips to tell her. Mrs Earnshaw slammed her book down, and the lips came slowly shut. But a quiet voice, from somewhere at the back, said slyly: 'To make that dimwit monitor. That spazz.'

Mrs Earnshaw went rigid, but too late. A gust of laughter swept across the class. The grim-faced teachers weathered it in silence. There was nothing else to do.

When it had finished, Louise said crisply: 'Simon, I don't want to talk to you in front of all these silly children. Come with me.'

He went reluctantly, red-faced and ashamed. Miss Shaw was red also, wishing she had not done this, wishing she had thought it through.

But as she saw the eyes of the children on him, hard with dislike, she became surer of one thing: if Simon was a bully, if he did lash out at people, he clearly had a reason. He would get more affection from the gerbil and the rabbits than he did from his 'friends' in class, she thought. Probably even from the tank of fish.

David Royle, she noticed as she left, was very careful not to meet her eye.

St Michael's was a small school, and before the afternoon was out the news – and the reaction – had spread like wildfire. It was not only Simon's class who were upset and scandalised, but all the children. Louise, in the playground, overheard whispered words, and had some shouted at her from round corners and through doors. Simon Mason was a simpleton, a fool, a wrecker.

At one point, as she walked towards a group with a tallish blonde girl in it, Louise knew that they were watching her. The group broke open, and the blonde girl was revealed as Anna Royle, with her friend Rebekkah and some hangers-on. They stared at her, heavy-eyed and almost sullen, until she stared straight back.

'Yes, Anna?'

Anna looked surprised.

'Nothing, Miss. We were just chatting, that's all. We're waiting for my brother.'

In fact, David had been the one to break the news to Anna, and Anna had been furious. To her, it was like an insult, a slap in the face.

'So she believes him,' she had hissed. 'She believes he's innocent and we're guilty! She's listened to the evidence and she's reached her verdict! Well, we'll see about that!'

'I don't know,' David had replied. 'Maybe she's just being nice to him.'

'Stupid! She thinks we're liars. She believes that little cheat, that little *bully*, and she thinks we're liars.'

'But he's such a little fool,' said Rebekkah, uncomfortably. 'He's such a nincompoop.'

'She'll find out,' said Anna. 'It's not our job to tell her, is it? She'll find out.'

Even in the staffroom, to Miss Shaw's disgust, there was a definite feeling that she'd made a bad mistake, although no one put it into words. It did not shake her confidence that she was right, but she took Simon to one side as soon as she got the chance and went over the rules and problems of the job in detail. After his initial fear, he was pleased and flattered now that he'd been chosen. He loved animals, he said, but they weren't allowed to keep one in their house.

'Now that's a point,' said Louise. 'We don't normally ask parental permission for this job, but you realise it will make you a bit late home, don't you? Settling them down only takes ten minutes every night, but if your mum and dad are expecting you?'

Something crossed his face, a shadow, and she regretted that she had not checked. Most of the children in the school lived with both their parents, but one never knew. Simon made no comment.

'That's all right, Miss,' he said. 'I often go and play before I go home to my tea. My . . . no one will miss me for a while.'

'Good. I was going to ask you to start today, if that's okay? Jump in at the deep end, as it were. Have you ever looked after animals before?'

He had not, so she gave him a quick run-down of the task. She took him to the pets' room, which was in the resources centre a small way from the main building, and showed him the bags of food, the cupboard where the clean water dispensers were, the sink to wash out dishes, the sack of shavings for when he cleaned the cages out, the cardboard tubs of fish-food. Simon stopped and stared for ages at the gerbil in its big clear plastic tank.

'Do you like him? He's lovely, isn't he?'

He turned his eyes slowly to her, as if he did

not want to take them off the gerbil, and they were filled with light.

'Yes,' he said, at last. 'He's smart.'

Louise was business-like once more.

'Now see that plastic top,' she said. 'That's the important thing. You take it off to feed him and to clean the cage, of course, but it *must* go back on, it's vital. Do you understand?'

'Yes,' he said. 'Please, Miss, can I touch him now?'

Miss Shaw gave a small laugh. His mind was on the gerbil, not on her.

'Simon, *concentrate*. Of course you can touch him, when you're monitor you can play with all the animals, but are you listening? What *must* you do when you're tending to the gerbil?'

'Put the lid on, Miss,' said Simon, instantly. 'Has he got a name, Miss? Can I give him one?'

'Well, officially he hasn't. Mrs Stacey thinks it's important that the animals are here to study, not to anthropomorphise. Do you know what that means, Simon? No, of course you don't!'

She let out another laugh, louder than the last one. Mrs Stacey, in her opinion, had some rather weird ideas, but she was the head, it was her privilege. Simon glanced at her for the laugh, but did not understand.

'But can I give him one?' he repeated. 'I want to call him Diggory, is that all right?'

'By me,' replied Louise, 'it's fine. I think Diggory's a splendid name, lovely. Look, we'd better

27

get back, you've missed half your schooling for the afternoon, you'll get me shot. Come back later, and make proper friends with him. But don't forget the lid, will you? Ever?'

'No, Miss.' He had his face pressed to the plastic, his breath steaming it over. 'Why, Miss? Would he run away? He won't want to run away when I'm in charge of him.'

His face had changed. It had a glow to it, a kind of shine that she had never seen before.

'I shouldn't think he would,' she said. 'But it's not him we've got to worry about, it's Butch. He's a lovely cat, but he's still a cat. He's an opportunist.'

Simon did not know the word, but he was thunderstruck.

'He wouldn't be so mean!' he gasped. 'Diggory's so . . . so *little*.'

'Yes. To Butch, he's breakfast-sized. Just don't leave the lid off, right?'

'I'd kill him!' said Simon. He looked genuinely upset. 'He's horrible! I'd kill him!'

'Simon!' Miss Shaw snapped the name out. His eyes came to hers, and cleared. He seemed close to tears.

'Simon,' she repeated, more gently. 'Cats are cats and gerbils are gerbils. They don't think, they're not human beings, they live on instinct. If Diggory got eaten by Butch it would not be Butch's fault, do you understand? It would be yours, for leaving off the lid. Not Butch's, not anybody else's, yours. Okay?'

28

Simon looked rebellious for several seconds. Then he nodded.

'I'll never leave the lid off, Miss,' he said. 'That's final.'

Brian, when he heard the children's 'vile reaction' to Louise's scheme, found it not at all surprising.

'I was amazed,' she said, not for the first time. 'Honestly, Brian, they were so horrible. They were baying like a pack of hounds. In all my years of teaching I've seen nothing like it.'

They were almost alone in the saloon bar of the pub that teachers used, which was not far from the school. Despite herself, Louise had hung around the premises until she had seen Simon leave the resources centre to go home. Mr Taylor, the caretaker, would have checked up afterwards; it was one of his last tasks each afternoon, but she wanted to be sure. Simon had been in with the animals for nearly half an hour, until she had started to get worried.

When she had seen him leave, though, the worries had evaporated. He still looked happy, as if he could walk on air. He stared all about him carefully, as if fearing ambush, and closed the centre door behind him. Louise had stepped into the shadow of the school kitchen so that he would not see her. She did not want him to think that she was spying on him, even if she was.

'Well,' said Brian, carefully, 'you know how cruel kids can be. They're like animals in some ways, aren't they? If you know what I mean.'

She looked at him quite frostily. Louise could be rather touchy sometimes.

'I'm not sure that I do.'

'Well,' said Brian. 'Let me put it this way. My aunt had a goose once that was born deformed. Its wings were back to front, it fell over if it tried to fly. She was quite fond of it, she kept it separate and fed it the best scraps. But as soon as she put it out among the flock of them, they attacked it unmercifully. She had to kill it in the end, before the others did. Her method was much quicker than a death by pecking.'

The pale oval face stayed serious.

'I hope you're not going to suggest we wring poor Simon's neck,' she said. 'Really, Brian, you're very lurid sometimes. They're children, not a flock of geese.'

'Of course,' said Brian. 'Although there's some of them could do with putting down! I just mean they're realistic, that's all. They don't pull their punches or pretend, like adults, they respond completely truthfully. If they perceive young Simon as a . . . as a . . .'

'Deformed goose? Oh come on, Brian, *really*.'

Then Louise sighed, and took a sip of her drink.

'I do know what you mean,' she said, 'and

that's the trouble. They call him Simple Simon, they call him worse. I suppose in their eyes he is like that. He's always falling over, anyway. He's the clumsiest boy I've ever seen. But it's not *his* fault. Is it?'

'No. It's not,' Brian answered. 'But it's not necessarily their fault if they react to what they see, either. You know yourself how hard it is to respond to children who aren't attractive. It's one of the most difficult things in teaching. If a kid's always got a snotty nose, or smells, or is just plain ugly . . . it's hard to like them. It's been proved, it's not just my idea, it's unfair but it's true. If it's hard for adults to get over it, it's probably impossible for kids.'

She did not argue; she swirled the ice cubes around the bottom of her glass. There was silence for a while.

'Well, anyway,' she said. 'If he's a bully I'll eat my hat. I've never seen a child respond like he did when I took him to the animals. I was really touched. What do you want to drink? Another pint of bitter, or a half?'

He settled for a half, thinking of his next statement while she was at the bar. The truth was, he thought, that – bully or just victim – Simon Mason was a hopeless case, a natural to get picked on. If he did lash out, as he'd said before, it was probably because of the tormenting, but so what? You could explain it that way, but not excuse it, could you? And he was quite prepared to bet that if Louise should give him trust, he'd mess it up somehow – terribly.

When Louise returned, they both started to speak at once. He gave her precedence.

'I was just going to say,' she said, 'that if Simon's *not* a bully—'

'Then Anna Royle is,' he finished for her. 'That's the conundrum, isn't it? And the problem.'

Louise raised her glass in mock salute.

'Precisely,' she said.

After tending to the animals, Simon ran home full of happiness to tell his mother. Even the access road to the chalkpit had no pull on him this afternoon. He felt different, keen. He felt sure that if he did it well, Miss Shaw would even let him keep the job – perhaps for good.

Unfortunately, his mother was less happy. At work it had been one of those days, and at the supermarket on her way home she had dropped six eggs. The first thing she noticed about her son was the mud on his white shirt, the second that he had no football kit.

'Simon! You're filthy. Where's your kit, it must need washing.'

The excited story about his gerbil friend died on Simon's lips. He looked at his own hands almost comically, as if they held the secret of the missing clothes and towel. His mind was blank. Football kit? What football kit?

'It must be . . . Mum!' he said, forgetting even that. 'Mum, they let me be the monitor! They let me feed the animals! I've got a gerbil!'

But Linda Mason could not respond. She bore down on him threateningly, her face closed off by anger.

'Where *are* they?' she demanded. 'It's weeks since those clothes were washed! Oh, Simon!'

He made to move away, and all at once she was out to hit him. He leapt behind the kitchen table.

'Stop it!' he shouted. 'It's not important! Stop it!'

Mrs Mason was in a bright fury. This was the part that Simon could never understand. It was as if she thought he did these things to upset her. As if he liked forgetting things. He wanted to go to her and plead with her, but he was afraid. Although she was not strong enough to really hurt, she hit him hard and he did not like it. Sometimes he lost his temper and they tore and scrambled like two cats. He hated it.

'I'm going out!' he said. 'I'm going out till you stop it! It's stupid, this, it's stupid, stupid!'

She lunged at him, and Simon ran into the passage, then out into the street. Mrs Mason did not follow, and a minute later he peered in through the kitchen window. She was standing by the cooker, one hand rested on the hob, white and tired. He knew that in another minute he could go in again, in safety, to his tea.

He wondered why he angered her so much. He thought about Diggory, how soft he felt, how lovely. Surely Butch wouldn't really hurt something so helpless? He wouldn't be so mean.

*

34

Anna and David Royle and Rebekkah walked home as usual, and they talked out their annoyance at the way things had happened right up to the Royles' back door. But in the kitchen, to their surprise, sat Rebekkah's mother, taking coffee with her friend.

'Hallo, Mum,' said Rebekkah cheekily. 'Who's going to make my tea!'

The women smiled and offered drinks, but soon made it clear that they were having one of their 'serious talks'. David's big mouth, apparently, had done more damage than expected.

'How's the bullying?' asked Mrs Royle, brightly. 'I told Avril what you said this morning in the car.'

'Oh, Mum!' said Anna. 'Do we look as if we've taken any stick?'

'Well, you haven't exactly got black eyes,' agreed her mother. 'But we are allowed to worry, you know.'

Rebekkah's mum was nodding.

'Some children can be very rough,' she said. 'Boys especially. You may think it's something to joke about, but if there is bullying going on, it's not a laughing matter. It's very prevalent these days, it's almost an epidemic.'

Rebekkah was uncrushed.

'I blame it on TV,' she said. 'If you let me watch *Grange Hill* and *Neighbours* I'm sure I'd be a better person! Really, Mum, you treat us just like babies. We can handle it.'

'Ah – handle what, though?' asked Mrs Royle.

She put her cup down carefully, as if she'd made a brilliant point. It was a habit people fell into in their house, thought Anna. Because her father was a lawyer, probably.

Suddenly, an idea came to her. Maybe they'd got it wrong, denying everything. Maybe there was a better tactic. She let go a little sigh, as if her mother had cleverly caught her out.

'Oh, well,' she said, 'we might as well admit it, I suppose. There is one kid.'

Rebekkah and David were more startled than the adults. David went round-eyed.

'Joke?' suggested Rebekkah, uncertainly. But Anna did not take up the chance to change her mind.

'No, seriously, Rebekkah. There *is* a minor problem. No point in denying it.'

The mothers were relieved and anxious, both at once. They leaned forward in their seats to learn the gruesome details.

'Go on,' said Mrs Royle. 'What boy? What sort of "minor problem"?'

'We *knew* there was something going on,' added Mrs Tanner. 'Gosh, getting you to tell us things is like getting blood from a stone.'

Rebekkah and David were eyeing each other. Neither knew what was going on, but David was being silently warned to keep his mouth shut.

'It's only stories,' said Anna. 'I mean, it honestly is nothing very serious. He's just been putting things around about us. That we've been . . . ragging him, you know.'

36

To her concern, both her mother and Rebekkah's got hot under the collar.

'But that's outrageous!' said Mrs Tanner. She had gone a fetching shade of pink.

'Who is this boy?' demanded Mrs Royle. 'Telling *lies* about you? Really, this is too bad, we'll have to talk to Mrs Stacey. What's his name?'

'No!' squeaked Rebekkah.

'Not yet,' said Anna, mildly. 'Oh Mum, you'll make me wish I hadn't told you.'

'David?' said his mother. 'You'll let me hear some sense. Who is this boy?'

David turned anxious eyes first on his sister, then her friend. He shook his head.

'Mum,' said Anna, 'you're not really being fair, are you? David's too young to understand. It's not fair on the boy either, is it, because we've got no proof.'

There was a pause while everyone considered this. Mrs Tanner looked at Anna with a new respect.

'Oh dear,' she said. 'Put like that you do sound right, I must say.'

'You're just like your father,' Mrs Royle sighed. 'Too fair-minded for your own good. And you, Rebekkah. We're lucky in our children, Avril, we're very lucky.'

What about me, thought David. I'm fair-minded too, aren't I? If those two are, at any rate . . .

Later, Anna explained why she had done it. Rebekkah understood immediately, but David found it rather harder.

37

'It's insurance,' Anna told him. 'Just in case Loo-roll believes the little beast. Or if anything else happens in future and he tries to drop us in it.'

David ran his fingers through his hair.

'But if he does, how can telling Mum about the last lot make any difference?'

Anna was exasperated.

'You're thick. Tell him, Rebekkah. I can't be bothered with the dimmy little squirt.'

They were in her bedroom, and she flounced off to the window to look out. The sun was on the hillside, and she could see the top section of the chalkpit cliffs, gleaming white. Rebekkah sat down on the bed.

'Look,' she said. 'If Simon told on us, and our mums already knew he would – what would they say when they heard he *had*?'

David thought hard for several seconds.

'I don't know,' he said.

'They'd say he'd made it up. They'd say we'd warned them that he would. They'd say that he was lying.'

'But he wasn't, was he? He didn't make it up?'

'But it hasn't happened yet! And he *has* been spreading stories! You ask our mums!'

David thought his brain was going to boil.

Rebekkah added, piously: 'Who could believe a terrible little liar like that? No one in their right mind.'

'And now we've got to punish him,' put in Anna. 'Someone's got to, haven't they?'

'Why?' asked David. 'What for?'

'Spreading stories!' cried Rebekkah. 'That's logic, David! It's a very useful thing.'

Smiling, Anna walked back into the middle of the room. She put her face right up to his.

'The boy's a menace, don't you understand? He needs a lesson teaching, quick.'

Rebekkah's face was radiant.

'And we're the ones to teach it him,' she said. 'Aren't we?'

Oh dear, thought David. Poor old Simple Simon.

CHAPTER SIX

Even before disaster struck for Simon, the headteacher of St Michael's had heard a hint of something going on. Mrs Stacey, a small and stocky woman with strong ideas, claimed that very few things happened within the wire fence that she was unaware of, and she was proud of it. Some teachers – among them Louise Shaw, her deputy – found this rather wearing.

Louise was standing in a corner of the playground the next morning talking to Mr Kershaw when they saw the head push through a doorway, glancing purposefully around her. It was near the end of break.

'Here's trouble,' she told Brian. 'Fifty pence gets you a pound someone's been blabbing about Simon and the animals. She'll have some daft objection, mark my words.'

Mr Kershaw was half-amused by her attitude. Considering that Mrs Stacey had helped her get promoted so quickly, he thought it bordered on ingratitude. However, he did find the head's tendency to interfere in everything less than funny sometimes.

'You know how it is,' he said. 'She doesn't like the working classes getting out of hand. She probably thinks that kids like Simon Mason eat gerbils for their breakfast.'

There was a grain of truth in this. Mrs Stacey was extremely fond of all the children in her care, but it was noticeable that she was fonder of some than others. Not many of the kids were working class or steeped in poverty, but those who were had no concessions made for them. The ethos was overwhelmingly for 'niceness' and 'respectability', and Mrs Stacey set enormous store by what she referred to in assembly as 'good behaviour and better manners – *attitude*!'

She had seen them, and the purposeful glances became a smile. She bustled through the knots of children rather like a small motor boat forging through a choppy sea. Brian, without making it too obvious, detached himself from Louise and set out towards the changing rooms. A boy called to him and he went to have a word. Louise set her face into a welcome.

'Louise, I've been looking for you!'

'Well, here I am. Was it something special?'

Mrs Stacey was totally unconscious of her bias against certain sorts of people, and Louise therefore found it difficult to actually dislike her. She could feel her irritation growing, however.

'Well, yes and no. I've probably got hold of the wrong end of the stick, in fact. It's a question of judgement, really.'

She looked at Louise enquiringly, as if she had

41

stated clearly what she had come to talk about. Although she'd guessed, Louise pretended that she had not.

'I'm sorry? What exactly . . . ?'

The children carried on their racing, swooping games. They were a well-behaved lot, no doubt about it. She noticed Simon Mason in a corner, quite alone.

'Little Simon,' cooed Mrs Stacey. 'I'm sorry, I thought you realised. Some of the others, in the staffroom. Well, of course, I'm not questioning your decision, but . . .'

'Simon? Oh, you mean the animals? I don't understand, Mrs Stacey. Is there any harm in that?'

'No harm? Of course, no harm. I just thought - well, several of the teachers – well, he is so very *clumsy*, isn't he? And . . . well, it would be unfortunate if anything went wrong, wouldn't it? Upsetting for *him*, never mind us old fogeys! We wouldn't want poor Simon to be upset, would we?'

Louise said crisply: 'Oh, I don't think we need worry much on that score, Mrs Stacey. He's not as daft as people like to paint him, in my opinion. And I'll keep an eye on things, naturally. Mr Taylor locks up every night, as well. I'll have a word with him.'

Mrs Stacey's attitude had hardened slightly.

'Correct me if I've got it wrong, but does the job not normally go to . . . No, what I mean is . . . well, it's a treat, isn't it? A reward for good behaviour?'

The women faced each other squarely. Louise could feel her temper rising, but Mrs Stacey kept hers under very tight control. Her lips tightened, that was all. Small lines radiated across the loose skin on her chin.

'I also heard an inkling of bullying,' she said. 'Now if that's true, Louise, it would be strange behaviour indeed to be rewarded with a monitorship.'

A buzzer went inside the school, and Louise glanced at her watch. To her relief it was the end of break. She pulled her whistle from the pocket of her skirt and gave a blast. It gave her a brief pause to catch her thoughts.

'It would indeed,' she answered. 'But I honestly have no firm evidence of bullying by Simon Mason, none at all. Whoever your informants are, you might tell them to be a bit more careful with their accusations, Mrs Stacey.'

Defence by attack, the good old principle. Mrs Stacey, caught on the wrong foot, coloured slightly.

'Louise.' Her voice was frosty. 'We have a fine tradition in St Michael's, for smartness, politeness, diligence – above all, respect for others. In some schools, I believe, bullying is all the rage these days, it's seen as quite the vogue. That is not, and that will not, be the case in my school. I trust you understand?'

'Naturally,' replied Louise, hiding her contempt. 'And if I catch anybody – if I have proof – it will be the worse for them. Quite frankly, I think some people might be just a little prejudiced against that child. I know how much you trust me, and I'm grateful for it. Please trust me in this.'

Mrs Stacey, knowing she had been left with little option, gave in gracefully.

'Of course I trust you, dear,' she said. 'You are my deputy, after all. But I must listen to the others, mustn't I – even when it seems they may be wrong?'

That was crafty, too, because it forced Louise to a small admission.

'They may not be completely wrong,' she conceded, stiffly. 'But I'm sure the risk's worth taking. I think the principle . . .'

She tailed off, and Mrs Stacey permitted herself a smirk.

'In the meantime,' she said, 'I'll say no more. You'd better get the stragglers in, hadn't you? But dear – I'll be keeping an eye on the situation, naturally. A close one.'

Simon liked the pets' room in the resources centre almost as much as he liked the pets themselves. It was small and darkish, with windows made of opaque, armoured glass, and smelled of rabbits, paint and chalk. The smell that rose from Diggory's tank when he took off the lid was wood shavings, sweet and piney. Gerbils, Miss Shaw had told him, did not need cleaning often, because they were desert animals who neither drank nor wet much. He touched him with a finger. Warm and lovely.

In his left hand, Simon still held the plastic lid.
His football kit and towel were crushed awkwardly against his side. As he juggled with everything, the towel slipped and his football shoes fell
out, one after the other. He had found the stuff
in the annexe to his classroom where he'd left it,
though by now it was scattered across the floor.
The kubutan had gone, but Simon did not mind
particularly. He was not feeling martial, in the
pets' room.

'Hang on, Diggory,' he told the gerbil. 'Let's
just get rid of this lot.'

He transferred the lid to his right hand, glancing round for somewhere to put it. In front of
him was a high shelf for powder paints and
poster colours. It needed a good clear-up, but it
would do. He balanced the piece of moulded
plastic carefully, then thought of Butch and
glanced around. 'Known tendencies,' Miss Shaw
had said. A friendly-looking tabby who would
gobble up small animals for snacks. In case he
might have sneaked in through the cat-flap (all
the doors in the centre had them, so that Butch
could not get trapped), Simon thought he'd better
check.

The little room was clear, though. Before return-
ing to the gerbil tank, Simon opened up the
rabbit-hutch and swept out the dirty floor-
covering into the special plastic bin. He put in
fresh, changed their water, gave them food. Then
it was the fish, which he found rather boring. By
the time he went back to the gerbil, Diggory

was standing on his hind legs, reaching up the glass wall, pink nostrils twitching. Simon slid both hands into the tank at once, moving them smoothly downwards so as not to frighten him. Making a clucking noise, he lifted Diggory to eye height, then kissed him on the nose.

The gerbil, as far as one could tell, was perfectly content. He did not wriggle, or try to get away. Simon rocked him in his cradled hands, crooning to him. He was aware that he was happy; he was filled with a sort of glowing pleasure. He dreamed of being good to Miss Shaw, doing special things for her, getting to have the gerbil – more or less – as his own. He could picture it as living in his house, in his bedroom, being his. He wondered if his mother would allow that.

But as he put Diggory back into the tank, and reached up to lift down the lid, it slipped sideways from the shelf. Simon grabbed at it, twitched it in his grasp, and knocked a tall tin of powder paint over. Inevitably, the top was open, inevitably, the packet inside was loose. A cascade of powder like a scarlet waterfall poured into the tank, much of it on to Diggory, who jumped in fright. As he did so, he gave off a cloud of bright red dust.

A small noise, a sort of moan, escaped from Simon's lips. As he reached to stop the cascade, the tank lid knocked another packet over. Royal-blue dust mixed with the scarlet, forming a pyramid on the piney shavings. Two or three paint tins fell off the shelf, bouncing on the table, then rolling along the floor to disappear.

Simon panicked. Terror clutched at him, terror at what Miss Shaw would say when she found out. All his dreams of being Diggory's master, all his fantasies of having him to cuddle and to hold were gone. A sob rose in his throat, into his mouth. He had to get away, he had to go, he had to hide.

But before he turned to flee, to stumble out of the dark room into the bright evening light, he put the gerbil's lid back on. He rocked it from side to side, he patted it to be certain it was firm.

That was one thing he would not forget. Ever.

Outside the playground, separated from the resources centre by a road and the high wire fence, David, Anna and Rebekkah watched as Simon ran away. David might have shouted but his sister stopped him.

'Did he see us?' she said, after a few moments.

'I don't know,' replied Rebekkah. 'I'm not sure. Gee, look at him go. What d'you think he's done?'

Simon was three hundred metres off, running fast.

'Search me,' said Anna. 'I think we ought to go and see, don't you?'

David hung back.

'Mr Taylor might come round. He's very strict, if you're not meant to be in there.'

Rebekkah checked her watch.

'Too early. He'll be at least ten minutes. He locks up the lab stuff first. That takes him ages.'

Anna was already half-way across the road.

'I vote we risk it,' she said. 'He'll have broken something, I expect. He always does.'

'What d'you reckon if he has?' said Rebekkah. 'Are we going to tell on him?'

Anna pushed some hair out of her eyes. She grinned.

'Think big,' she said, mysteriously. 'Think big . . .'

When Mr Taylor came to the resources centre twenty minutes later, Butch was lying in a shaft of sunlight just outside the door. As the man approached, the fat, sleek tabby rolled on to his back, and stretched out all four legs, and sighed noisily. Mr Taylor bent, crooking strong fingers underneath the furry chin, and scratched. Butch, purring like a motor mower, rolled into a comfortable ball.

'What a life, eh?' asked the caretaker, of nobody at all. 'You're a lucky devil, Butch. I envy you.'

By next morning, when he told Miss Shaw what he had later found, Mr Taylor's envy had become regret. The cat, they both agreed, could not be blamed in any way – you could not argue with its nature. He was even surprisingly nice about the human culprit, although the scattering of paints all over the floor and the up-ended tin of fishfood seemed unnecessary. Perhaps, he asked – he half suggested – the boy had merely panicked; knocked something over, then clumsily made things worse? Would that be possible? Miss Shaw, with heavy heart, agreed it could.

Twenty minutes later, when Brian Kershaw came jogging to the gate, she had still come to no firm conclusion about the disaster. He stopped, hardly panting after his morning run, and asked her what was going on. In a few crisp sentences she told him, and Mr Kershaw did not even smile. He did not even say 'I told you so'.

'Oh dear,' he said. 'Your little lad has let you down. That's sad.'

She searched his face but found no malice there.

'Just like you predicted, Brian. But I must admit I still don't understand it.'

The games teacher scanned the lines of children making for the gate. Simon was not among them.

'No,' he said. 'It does seem odd. And he messed the place up, too? He must be pretty stupid, if you don't mind me saying so. What did our Beryl say?'

'I almost didn't tell her,' said Louise. 'That was Bill Taylor's idea, he doesn't like her, either. I lied a bit, in fact. I said the gerbil had escaped, but not that stuff had been chucked around. Bill said he'd clean it up before she had a chance to check. He didn't mind.'

'Nice bloke. I suppose she gave you her "crime and punishment" speech?'

'She did. She brought it all in – sloppiness, unpunctuality, his inability to grasp the simplest instruction. Even if he left the lid off by mistake he was guilty, that was the drift of it. People like Simon Mason just don't *try*.' She sighed. 'I told her I took full responsibility, of course. And that I'd buy another gerbil. She said she was going to mention it in assembly.'

'Oh glory! What did you do?'

Louise glanced at her watch. They were down to stragglers now.

'I blew my top. I told her we didn't even know the facts. I hope Simon comes up with something good by way of explanation. A doctor's note would be the safest. Guilty but insane!'

The playground was almost empty. Assembly was due to start at any time. Louise had a mental picture of the head, smug and dumpy, crowing to the school about what a bad boy Simon was.

'Oh dear, it's so depressing,' she went on. 'And now he won't turn up, and then what do I do? I wish I'd never given him the benefit of the doubt.'

Louise turned towards the school. Simultaneously, Brian pointed.

'Look,' he said. 'Behind that van. I do believe the wanderer's returned.'

'Thank goodness.' She stepped on to the pavement, waving her arms and calling.

'Simon! Simon! Come on quick, you're late!'

Simon showed himself, but did not come closer. If anything he looked as if he would run away.

'Simon!' repeated Louise. 'I won't do anything. I want to talk.'

Brian raised his arms out from his sides.

'You might as well come, son. Because if you don't I'll have you in two hundred metres. Want a race?'

'Oh, Brian,' muttered Louise.

But it worked. After a few more moments, Simon walked towards them. As he got close they saw his face was wet with tears, and Mr Kershaw tactfully went through the gates and off towards the school.

'I'm sorry, Miss,' said Simon.

She cleared her throat.

'Go to the lavs and wash your face,' she said. 'Come to my room at playtime. Run!'

Even on the clear, flat tarmac, Simon managed to trip . . .

CHAPTER EIGHT

On the way to school, he had gone into the chalkpit hoping something would occur to him to make things better. So silent was he in his pondering that after a few minutes two young rabbits hopped out into his view and continued feeding. Simon, for a moment, forgot his troubles and enjoyed their company. Then it all came back.

The night before, he had decided to tell his mum about it, risking her swings of mood. In fact, she had been quite happy and relaxed, but he had not known how to start. It would sound too stupid, too familiar – breaking things, spilling things, knocking things off tables. It just wasn't worth it.

He had left the chalkpit in time not to be late to school, but the sight of Miss Shaw and Mr Kershaw standing in the gateway had unnerved him. He had spent a lot of time convincing himself that his crime was not so terrible as all that, even if it did mean he'd be sacked as monitor, but if they were waiting as a pair it must be really serious. He had cried a little in the night, unable to go to sleep for ages, and the tears began again.

He only went forward when there was clearly no escape.

By playtime he was calmer, more resigned. He had sat unthinking and unseeing through his lessons, working it all out. He would offer, naturally, to clean up the spilled paint after school or in his dinner-hour, and he would tell Miss Shaw straight out that he knew he'd lost his job. But he would apologise, and ask her if he could possibly see Diggory again, hold him sometimes, if she could spare the time to go into the pets' room with him. Miss Shaw was nice, there was no doubt of that. He convinced himself that she did not frighten him.

Consequently – rather to her surprise – Simon was not cowed when he stepped into her room, he was neither tremulous nor crying. The smile he managed threw her off her balance, rather; it startled her. Louise had had her own problems with this case.

'Well,' she said. 'Your remorse was short-lived, wasn't it?'

Simon did not understand the word, nor precisely what she meant. The tone got to him, though, it cut deep into his store of confidence.

'Miss?'

Louise felt annoyed with herself. The whole thing was annoying, a rotten nuisance. She shook her head, impatiently.

'Oh, never mind. Look, I haven't got all day to waste. Just tell me why you did it.'

Simon swallowed. A small edge of fright started to grow in him.

'Please, Miss, it was an accident.'

His smile had gone. His face was blank.

'Oh, come on! What sort of accident is that?'

The fear was growing. She wasn't being nice at all. She was positively unfriendly.

'Miss?'

'To leave the lid off? How could that be accidental, Simon?'

He had a mental picture of the paint tin falling over. The lid was on it when it started, sort of. Loose, because it opened, but definitely on.

'I didn't, Miss!' he said. 'It was loose. I just knocked it over and it went everywhere. The paint.'

She was puzzled, but she was cross. She thought he was making it up, trying to wriggle out of it.

'What are you talking about? I'm not on about the paint, Simon, I'm on about the gerbil. You're surely not denying that was carelessness?'

He blinked.

'I didn't touch the gerbil, Miss,' he said. 'What's happened?'

'Simon,' snapped Miss Shaw, 'you're being silly, of course you touched him. You left the lid off, didn't you? Unfortunately, the gerbil's d—'

There was a look of horror on his face that made her stop. Careless or not, clumsy or not, he clearly did not know what he'd done, the consequences of his actions. She was afraid he was going to burst out crying.

'Well,' she put in quickly. 'We don't know that, of course. What we *do* know—'

'Diggory! Diggory's dead?'

He was taking in a huge and shaking breath. His face was white.

'No!' she said, more urgently. 'He probably isn't anything like that, he's probably run away. He'll be hiding somewhere in the resources centre.'

But Simon's face had changed again. He was excited, eager.

'I saw them!' he shouted. 'Hanging round outside! That Anna Royle and her brother and that girl! I saw them, Miss! They must have done it, Miss!'

Two red spots had grown on his cheeks, big red splotches. Anger and excitement.

'Simon!' said Miss Shaw. 'How dare you make things up! You forgot the lid and that is bad enough! You even admit you threw the paint about! Now don't tell silly, wicked lies!'

'I didn't throw it about! I knocked it over! It went in Diggory's cage and I was scared! But I left the lid on! I did, I did!'

'You did not!'

The red had taken over all his face. He was red from ear to ear, scarlet. Louise stared at him, trying to read the truth. Even if he was lying – and she guessed he was – she could forgive him. She could understand, in part.

'Simon,' she said, quite gently, 'I think you'd better stop. I don't think for a moment that you saw those children, I don't think for a moment there was anyone else involved. But Mr Taylor's very kindly done the clearing up and ... and, who knows, Diggory might turn up himself. Surprise us all.'

She had been going to punish him, tell him at least, coldly and clearly, that he was not the monitor any more. She found she did not have the heart. He was desolate, forlorn.

'Miss,' he said. 'I did see them. I did, Miss.'

He stood in front of her, untidy, unattractive. He could see that she did not believe him, still. He did not try again.

After a moment he said quietly: 'Do you think he will, Miss? Diggory?' New tears were welling in his eyes. 'He's not really dead, is he? Not really?'

'If he is,' said Louise Shaw, 'it will be because the lid was left off, won't it?'

That was all the punishment that she could manage. It left her instantly ashamed.

There was no real doubt in her mind, but Louise decided that she had to put it to the girls and David Royle. It would be annoying if they *had* been in the area – however innocently – because it muddied the waters. The simple fact, she knew, was that Simon had been in a funk, and had seen the chance to maybe shift the blame. She was interested to note, though – when she cornered them at lunch-time in the playground – how shifty David instantly became. Anna and Rebekkah only smiled.

'Hallo, Miss,' said Rebekkah. 'Slumming?'

'Collecting evidence, more like,' said Anna coolly.

David shot a startled glance at his sister, and Louise wondered if she had made a mistake. Nobody knew about the gerbil, she and Mr Taylor had made very sure of that.

'Whatever do you mean, Anna?' she asked.

'About the incident in the playing field,' Anna replied. 'We were telling the truth, you know, Miss Shaw. Simon Mason's always bashing people.'

Louise had lost the advantage, but she had to carry on.

'Did you see him last night, David?' she asked.

Anna answered.

'No, we didn't. What, after school?'

Rebekkah read her face and knew that they'd been spotted. She moved quickly.

'Yes we did, Anna. Don't you remember? As we were going down Peel Road. He was in the playground, wasn't he?'

Anna nodded, as if she'd just recalled it.

'Oh, that's right, Miss, we did. We were a long way off, though. Too far for him to chuck a rock at us.'

'Very amusing. Where, in the playground? What was he doing? David?'

David licked his lips. But the girls did not seem nervous, so he spoke.

'By the resources centre. I think he'd just come out. I think he'd been looking at the animals.'

Rebekkah gave her pert grin. It bordered on

the frankly cheeky. Okay, thought Louise – shock tactics.

'He said he'd seen you. After he'd left the animals. After he'd left the gerbil safe and sound, with its lid on. Does that sound right?'

David hunched his shoulders, shuffling his feet. Louise wished she had him on his own. Too late now, unfortunately. It was Anna who replied.

'Unless he'd had an accident,' she said. 'Any normal kid would leave the lid on, wouldn't they?'

'What do you mean, an accident?' said Louise, sharply. 'What sort of accident?'

Anna did not answer her, just looked. Her face was calm, serious and concerned. Louise felt a fool, as if she'd been outmanoeuvred.

'Was there an accident?' said Rebekkah. 'Something must have happened, mustn't it? Or why would you be asking us?'

'Nothing happened,' said Louise, and regretted it. 'Nothing I want to talk about out here. There will be an announcement, I expect.'

David started grinning. Tension over! His sister's face remained serious.

'Oh dear,' she said. 'I hope it's nothing awful, Miss. Everybody wondered, when you made him monitor. Is the gerbil okay? Oh, he's so sweet and cuddly! Is he all right, honestly?'

Louise turned away.

To Brian, later, she was able to let her anger show. She got him in a quiet corner and practically danced with fury.

'They were so cool! So self-contained, so *insolent*. Almost from the start they put me on the defensive. It was like a double act – with David as the stooge!'

'They're smart,' said Brian. 'Anna in particular. She's one of those infuriating ones – everything she does she does well.'

'This wasn't just smart, though, it was ... *rehearsed*! To show Simon up in the worst light possible!'

Brian was dubious.

'Mm,' he went. 'Well, that sounds ... Well, maybe they're not being brilliant so much as ... Well, maybe they're just telling you the truth. As they see it, of course.'

'Which is?'

'Well, as they see it ...' He bit on the bullet. 'Well, he is a liar, isn't he? You haven't changed your mind on that?'

Louise bit her lower lip. She pondered.

'Honestly,' said Brian. 'The evidence is all on Anna's side, it's difficult to disagree with that. Maybe they think you're going soft on him. Maybe they're right ...'

Louise still said nothing. Brian studied her face.

'He is a liar, and a bully, isn't he?' he said. 'However sorry you might feel for him. If you let him get away with that, who could blame them for being furious?'

Who could blame them indeed? Despite the calm way they had dealt with Miss Shaw, Anna and Rebekkah felt no triumph. They were, in fact, getting really angry with the situation. The further on it went, strangely, the more they blamed Simon Mason. This part David did not understand.

'It's getting out of hand,' said Anna. 'We're being questioned now, like common criminals. She'll be giving him a medal next!'

'The cheek of the woman,' agreed Rebekkah. 'Trying to trick us into admitting something. She must think we were born yesterday.'

They were in a corridor which was getting busy. Rumours about the gerbil were inevitably beginning to spread, and friends who had seen Miss Shaw talking to them in the playground were asking questions. They were having none of it.

'Don't you breathe a word to anyone,' Anna told her brother fiercely. 'He's got us in it deep enough already. We know nothing about any-thing, okay?'

61

David nodded, although he thought they were missing a golden opportunity. At least five kids had whispered to him that the gerbil was no more, and blamed Simon Mason quite cheerfully. He could not see why they didn't build on that, make sure he got *all* the stick.

'The worst thing,' said Rebekkah, 'is that old Loo-roll obviously isn't going to punish him. She's not going to do *anything* to him.'

Anna agreed.

'It's extraordinary,' she said. 'She makes him monitor when everybody *knows* what'll happen, and when it does, she lets him off scot-free. It can't be good for discipline, can it?'

'And the trouble is,' Rebekkah added, 'that he's getting us farther in it all the time. First he lies to her about what happened on the playing fields, then he tells her we were involved in the gerbil thing. And she believes him!'

And it's true, thought David! He said nothing, though. Both his sister and Rebekkah had got very bitter about all this, very dangerous. They made him rather frightened, in a way.

They had reached the end of a corridor where they had to separate. The girls were going off to geography, while David had library studies. It was the last session before dinnertime.

'What worries me,' said Anna, stopping at the junction, 'is where it could end up. I think we ought to have a word with Simple Simon, double-quick. I think he needs a warning.'

'A pre-emptive strike,' said Rebekkah. She

smiled, pushing twists of hair out of her eyes. 'Mouth shut or else.'

'What if he tells?' asked David. His voice was small and frightened.

His big sister took his earlobe between her fingers, quite gently. Slowly she increased the pressure until it began to really hurt.

'He won't.'

At lunch-time Mrs Stacey sent a message to Louise's room, telling her to come along and talk. Louise pretended that she had not got the note, and went out to her car. It was time, she had decided, to speak to Simon's mother. She did not bother to try and find a phone number. This interview would be better face to face.

Louise did not know the part of town the Masons lived in very well, but she had a map. The streets were surprisingly broad, and the houses all had long gardens at the back. Behind them, the grassy chalklands spread back and up-wards to a near horizon. The great white scar of the chalkpit could be seen over to her right as she faced Simon's door. The house was well-painted, neat, peaceful. Somehow, she had expected some-thing . . . worse.

'Mrs Mason? I'm Louise Shaw, Simon's deputy headteacher. I think we met once, at the school.'

Mrs Mason was startled, and coloured slightly. She pulled the front door to behind her, as if she wanted to hide the passageway. Louise wondered if there was somebody else inside.

'Did we? I'm sorry, but I don't remember.'

'Oh, that's all right,' began Louise, in a falsely jolly voice. But a worried look had grown on Mrs Mason's face.

'Is he all right? There's nothing wrong, is there? Not an accident, or anything?'

'Nothing,' said Louise. 'Honestly. It's . . . there's something I'd like to talk about, that's all. Something fairly complicated. It would really help me if we could . . . you know, go inside. Would that be possible?'

For a brief moment, she thought that Mrs Mason would say no. It was a shock to realise she would not have known how to handle that. But Mrs Mason nodded, although the worried look had hardly left her face.

'I've not got long,' she said. 'I'm working down at Baxter's at the moment. I've got to be back in half an hour.'

'I could drive you, maybe?'

Mrs Mason shook her head. 'Don't you know the area?' she asked. 'It's two hundred yards away.'

Feeling rather silly, Louise followed her into the living room. It was cluttered, untidy, but no worse than her own flat. There was nobody else. Simon's mother had been collecting dirty clothes up for a wash. She pointed to a chair, and Louise sat.

'Coffee? Tea? Smoke if you want to, I don't mind.'

'I don't, thanks. And I'm all right for the

moment, not thirsty. Look, Mrs Mason, I'd better start. You're being very kind, but in two minutes you might want to throw me out.'

Mrs Mason stared at her. Louise could hear a clock, and quickly found the source. A small electric alarm, on the mantelpiece. Linda Mason sat down, still staring.

'Has he been in trouble?' she asked. 'Has he been bad again? What is it this time? Stealing? Breaking things? Fights?'

Louise was shocked, but she seized the opportunity.

'If I said bullying, would that surprise you, Mrs Mason? Don't get me wrong, I'm not at all sure he has been, but . . . but would it be a possibility?'

Mrs Mason, she realised, looked tired. Her face was pale, and had many lines. She also realised that they were probably the same age, or near enough. She hoped to God she did not look like that to other people.

'Bullying.' She sighed. 'No, it wouldn't surprise me all that much. Is it true? I mean, have you got proof, or is it just a guess? I suppose there's been complaints?'

The reaction seemed very odd to Louise. In her experience, parents never believed bad of their own children. They defended them quite wildly, however wrong they were. This was rather worrying.

Because she had not answered, Mrs Mason carried on. Her voice was calm, almost dull, as she discussed her son.

'He is a problem child. There's no point in denying it. At his last school he got in a lot of trouble and he showed me up to be a fool as well. He used to tell me he was bullied, that the others picked on him, but then the teachers caught him out. He used to throw kids' shoes and things down the lavatories, their gym shoes, you know. He swore black was white it wasn't him and one day a teacher hid in the lavs and watched him do it. He never would say why, though.'

Louise waited. She guessed she'd hear more that way.

'You see,' said Mrs Mason, 'it's not that I don't . . . you know, love him. I am his mum, aren't I? But sometimes I don't know what to do. He's sort of slow, you know, he's lumpy, he's not got any enthusiasm for anything. He's not very good at anything, quite honestly, is he? And he's not got any friends, that's the worst thing. There isn't anyone he knocks about with.'

'But he loves animals!' cried Louise. To her surprise she realised she wanted to defend Simon, wanted to convince his mother of his hidden worth. She also realised she could hardly talk about Diggory the gerbil, in the circumstances.

'Maybe if we . . .' she began. She stopped. She thought she must be going red.

Simon's mother said: 'He did mention something. The other night, about a . . . I can't remember. Some sort of animal, I think. But then we had a little row, he'd forgotten his kit or something. That's another thing, he's so forgetful. I can't help thinking he does it on purpose, sort of. Just doesn't care. Sometimes I do get angry, I admit that.'

This woman is too honest, thought Louise. It would be better for her son if she behaved like all the others, blindly defending. She wished she had not come.

'The truth is,' said Mrs Mason, 'I don't know *what* the truth is about anything. I've told him and I've told him – tell lies once and you'll never be believed again. I know he's told lies in the past and I daren't ask him now. He wouldn't tell me, anyway. He never talks about his troubles any more.'

Rather abruptly, Louise got to her feet. She glanced at her watch, flustered.

'I'd better go. It's getting rather late. Thank you for talking, Mrs Mason. It's been very useful.'

Linda Mason also stood, startled.

'But you haven't told me anything. About the bullying. Was it serious? Was anybody hurt? Is anything going to happen to my Simon?'

'Not at all,' said Louise, briskly. She made for the front door. 'It wasn't serious and there's no evidence directly linking him. I'd be very surprised if you hear another word about it.'

'Look, I'm worried!' said Mrs Mason. She was surprised, also, at the speed of Miss Shaw's departure. 'Don't get me wrong, he's a good boy Simon, but ... Are you sure that ... ? He did kick a boy once, at his other school, a Kung Fu thing. He does like martial arts.'

67

Louise was at her car, fumbling to get the key into the lock. Simon is a little boy, she wanted to shout, this isn't serious, this is children's games.

'Really,' she said. 'Mrs Mason. I think I've jumped the gun. Talk to Simon, if you can, but nothing terrible has happened, I promise you. I was just trying to find things out. Nothing bad has happened and nothing will. I'm sure of it.'

Oh dear, she thought, as she turned the first corner. I'm not sure of anything any more.

Anna, Rebekkah and David cornered Simon at the start of lunch-time, and they went in hard. Brian Kershaw, who had noticed him standing by the pavilion, watched from a distance of three hundred metres as the two girls and the smaller boy walked up to him. He could not see exactly what took place, but there was no doubt about the sudden rush by Simon Mason on to David Royle, the flailing arms, the yellow plastic box that flew into the air, scattering sandwiches and a blue and purple flask.

'Hoi!' roared Brian. 'I saw that, Mason!'

Neither Simon nor the others heard him above the lunch-time din. As he ran towards them, they began to race for the pavilion, Simon first, Rebekkah Tanner, then tall, blonde Anna. David Royle was on his knees among the sandwiches, salvaging his dinner from the mud. Brian, throwing him a glance as he rocketed past, thought he might be crying.

Behind the pavilion, Simon most definitely was

not. He was red in the face with anger, his face was ugly and contorted. He was standing with his back to a wall, a large flint boulder in his hand drawn back for hurling. His mouth was open, flecked with wet, emitting a gasping, sobbing sound. Mr Kershaw hardly noticed the two girls, only the danger they were in if Simon should let fly the jagged rock.

'Drop!' he yelled. 'Drop it, boy!' But before Simon had the chance the teacher was on him, had knocked the flint to the ground, was shaking his arm violently.

'You fool!' he said. 'You silly little fool! You're going to hurt somebody soon! Control yourself!'

Simon was gazing at him, blinking, his mouth still wetly open. Mr Kershaw dropped his wrist, almost threw it from him, and turned away. He strode out into the open playing field without another word, his face closed against the crowds of kids who were running up to see the fun. He was not even really conscious if Anna and Rebekkah were still there.

They were. After the teacher had gone, and before Simon could run from the approaching hordes of noseys, Anna walked up to him and laughed in his face.

'That was nothing,' she said. 'We want to see you after school, in the field down by the brick-yard. You'd better be there, Spazzie.'

'No,' he said, not shouting now, the rage all died away. 'No.'

'Oh yes,' said Anna. 'You needn't be afraid, we're not going to hurt you.'

'There's going to be a trial,' Rebekkah said. 'We're going to listen to the evidence, and find you guilty, and sentence you. That's all.'

Then the other kids came racing round to see if they could get a thump at him, and Simon ran. Anna and Rebekkah, well-satisfied, went to find little David.

CHAPTER TEN

Louise arrived back at St Michael's too late for the headteacher to conduct the bitter interview that she had planned. Tight-lipped, she put it off until the end of afternoon school. But her anger did show through, quite clearly.

'Miss Shaw,' she said. 'This must be sorted out. I will no longer tolerate such behaviour in my school.'

Miss Shaw indeed! Louise felt her chest tighten angrily.

'What behaviour?' she said.

'There are rumours flying everywhere. All the children say Simon Mason killed the gerbil. They say he poured paint everywhere, wrecked the resources centre.'

'What nonsense!' replied Louise robustly. 'What does Mr Taylor say? It isn't true.'

The buzzer was clattering on the wall above Mrs Stacey's head. Passing children – teachers too – had looked at them with open curiosity.

'Nevertheless,' snapped the headteacher, 'I want it sorted out. I want an explanation from you. At break.'

'I'm sorry, I won't be free at break. I—'

'At final bell, then! In my room!' She paused, momentarily. 'There are standards in this school, Miss Shaw, and they must be maintained. I expect you to maintain them, as my deputy.'

She turned and steamed off, her shoulders and her bottom swaying aggressively. Ten seconds later Brian appeared beside Louise. He had been watching from a distance.

'I'll swing for her,' said Louise flatly. 'She'll drive me up the wall.'

Brian's face was troubled.

'Look, Louise,' he said, 'I've got some news for you. Bad news. About your Simon Mason.'

Her stomach hollowed.

'Go on.'

'I caught him out at dinner. He attacked the Royle boy. Snot and sandwiches everywhere.'

'Oh no! Oh, Brian . . . was it serious?'

'He used a rock again. It could have been appalling.'

Mrs Stacey, it quickly became clear, wanted to make an issue out of it. The two women faced each other across her desk, but it might as well have been the Grand Canyon, they were so far apart in attitudes.

She had spoken to Mr Taylor, she told Louise, and she had gained an admission from him that paint had been thrown about. She had spoken to several of the children at random during the afternoon and been told – clearly and categorically – that Simon Mason had left the lid off the gerbil cage and that Butch had eaten the animal.

'This,' she said, importantly, 'is not what you told me, Louise.'

'It is not what I told you,' she replied, 'because it is not what I knew at the time. I still do not know that it is the truth. Children, in my experience, don't make the most reliable of witnesses.'

Mrs Stacey was impatient.

'Some children do. One can tell the ones who lie habitually, can't one? And Mr Taylor has confirmed it. Isn't that enough?'

'Confirmed that Butch did the eating?' Louise could not keep a small note of sarcasm from her voice. 'I should have thought only Butch could—'

Mrs Stacey's face went red. Her lips tightened and she drew in a sharp breath through her nose.

'Louise! I insist that you take this seriously! Here we have a boy who is a liar and a bully! Off your own bat you gave him every chance, and he behaved abominably! Still you defend him, and now you stoop to silly jokes! I will not have it!'

They stared at each other, tight with anger. Louise regretted her sarcasm, but she could not say so now. What *could* she say? That she was not convinced? That there was still no evidence?

But Mrs Stacey had not finished.

'Before you go on,' she said, 'perhaps I ought to tell you of another thing. This too is rumour, or hearsay at least, but you ignore it at your peril. There was another incident at lunch-time.

73

Your Simon attacked the Royle boy. Mr Kershaw had to intervene. I am due to speak to Brian in a few minutes, and if he confirms it, I intend to take some action. This is bullying, Louise, and I am going to stamp it out. That is a promise.'

All Louise could think of, for the moment, was that Simon had been called 'hers' again – the second time. Odd, she thought, how people pinned their problems on to someone else.

'Mrs Stacey,' she began, after a pause. 'Simon Mason has got problems, I'm well aware of that. But . . .'

There was a knock, and Mrs Stacey moved immediately to the door and opened it. It was Brian, looking rather sheepish. Bang went Louise's chance to have a quiet word with him before the interview.

'Ah, Brian,' said the headteacher. 'Do come in. Louise is leaving now.'

As she passed him, Louise tried to mouth a message. He tried to read her lips, pretending not to. They said, quite plainly, 'don't tell'.

But as she walked along the corridor, she knew that she was clutching at straws. How could he not tell? What else could he say?

It was hopeless.

Simon, throughout the afternoon, had only one thought in his head – escape. He paid even less attention to anything than usual, and jumped like a startled rabbit when Mrs Earnshaw shouted at him. He worked out plan after plan for getting away at home-time, and did not think that any of them would work. Anna and Rebekkah – with a little help from David – would have all routes covered. They would grab him and frog-march him to the field and fill him in. This time there was no escape.

Strangely, it was easy. When the buzzer went he ran for the door, ignoring Mrs Earnshaw's outraged shout. He ploughed through the children trickling out of other class-rooms to collect their coats from the passageway, and he was in the inner yard within twenty seconds. He left the main gate so fast he almost ran underneath a car, despite the outer barrier that was meant to stop such things happening, and by the time the first knot of children came on to the pavement he was two hundred metres down the road and going well. He arrived at his own front door half an hour earlier than he could remember ever having done before.

His mother was at home, and she was surprised to see him. She too had spent the afternoon worrying, and had hurried back from Baxter's the moment she was free. She had decided to make him a nice tea, beefburgers and chips and the vile tinned peas that were his favourites. Miss Shaw's visit had upset her horribly, and she had decided to be calm and nice, and talk it through with Simon sensibly, find out what had been happening. The moment they set eyes on each other, it started to go wrong.

The trouble was that Simon wanted to tell her,

too. He wanted to tell about the way Anna and Rebekkah bullied him, about the way Butch had killed his gerbil, about how he'd been driven to a violent rage at dinnertime and spilled David Royle's sandwiches. He would never have admitted it, but he wanted to fall into her arms and sob his heart out.

She stood in front of him, pale-faced in her apron, an open tin of peas in her hand. His lip began to wobble and his mouth began to gape. He tried to speak, to get it out, but only made an ugly noise that juddered in his throat.

'I've been,' he said. 'I've been . . . These kids . . .'

As his mother watched, a small run of snot appeared from his left nostril, and grew into a bubble. He wiped his jumper sleeve across his face and left a trail across his cheek. Something in her broke.

'You've been bullying!' she shrieked. She raised her hand in a sudden gesture and peas flew from the open tin in a glutinous, slimy mass. They fell on to the cooker and the work surface, and dripped on to the floor. 'Your teacher's been and told me everything! You've let me down again! Oh Simon, why do you do it? Why?'

Simon's eyes were now wide like his mouth. He was full of horror.

'What teacher?' he gasped. 'Who?'

'Never mind who! It could have been any one of them, couldn't it? You've been lying to me, you've been telling lies again! What have you been doing, you bad, bad boy!'

'Nothing!' he yelled. 'Nothing! Nothing! Nothing! Why don't you believe me, why do you believe that old cow! It's kids, not me! They've been getting me, not me getting them!'

'Liar! That woman drove here! She said you'd been up to your usual tricks! Bullying!'

It could only be Miss Shaw. Mrs Mason slammed the tin down and Simon flinched, backing himself up to the door frame. She touched her hair, leaving a large green splash of pea juice, and he slid further along the wall. He was not frightened, he was still full of horror. It could only be Miss Shaw, and he'd called her an old cow, and he had not meant it. Somehow, against all the odds, he had thought that she was on his side. He'd been wrong.

Any danger of his mother hitting him was past. She stood unmoving, with peas and slime all down her arm. She was exhausted.

'Why do you do it, love?' she said. 'Why do you do it to me, Simon?'

He turned and ran away, out into the street. He did not go to the chalkpit, but up the hill the pit was carved out of. He crawled into a bush and looked out at the sea from deep inside its thorny heart. There were some sailing boats with multi-coloured sails, but they did not interest him.

He thought of Diggory.

At the chosen field, Anna and Rebekkah had their court case, and sentenced Simon Mason – in his absence – to a real good battering. David, who was certain now that everything would end up badly, spent the whole trial muttering and sulking.

'If you won't take part, shut up!' said Anna, at one point. 'You're spoiling it.'

'You'll end up in the dock as well,' warned Rebekkah. 'For you we might bring back the death sentence. Stretch a point.'

'Stretch a neck!' said Anna. 'Look, David, it's all quite legal, this. You can try people if they jump their bail.'

David secretly thought that if they used their brains, they could have found where Simon had jumped his bail *to* pretty easily. He'd have put good money on him skulking in the chalkpit, where they knew he played alone a lot, having stalked him on occasion. But he was having nothing more to do with the so-called trial, if he could help it. Whatever fun there'd been in baiting Simon had dwindled long ago.

There was not that much fun, indeed, even for the girls. It had not occurred to them that he would not come, they had not dreamed he might be brave enough to dare defy them. When the sentencing was over they joined David.

'He'll regret it,' Anna said. 'I vote we give him extra for annoying us. Wasting our time. Three Chinese burns, until he cries. What's up with you, you little bore?'

David was kicking at the turf. His face was troubled.

'Look, this is daft,' he said. 'We're in enough trouble as it is, killing the gerbil. Let's leave him alone.'

The girls bore down on him, pushing him backwards towards the bushes.

'What?' said Rebekkah. '*Who* killed the gerbil? *We* didn't kill the gerbil, did we?'

'We left the lid off, didn't we? If anyone finds out—'

Anna was jabbing him in the chest.

'If anyone finds out,' she said, timing the words to finger-jabs, 'we'll know who split on us, won't we? Just keep your mouth shut, David.'

'You're stupid, anyway,' added Rebekkah. 'We only did things because we had to, didn't we? Simple Simon hit Anna, and got away scot-free. He got rewarded, actually. Is that what you call justice? Is that what you call fair?'

Not fair on the poor old gerbil, either, David thought. But his sister's jabs were hurting him. They were sharp.

'Well?' demanded Anna. 'Is it?'

'No,' said David.

'No. Good. And don't you dare forget it, will you? Who killed the gerbil, David?'

'Simon.'

'Good. And tomorrow – he's going to pay.'

Simon, if he had known how to get away with it, would not have gone to school next morning. When his mother called up the stairs he did not wake up, and when she came into the room she had to shake him.

'Simon! Simon! What's up with you?'

He slowly came out of a deep sleep. His head was heavy, as if he had the flu. A small flicker of fear came to him the instant he was awake. The night had been full of nasty, fearful dreams, to do with climbing out of the estate by the steepest roads, but always falling back. He had lain awake for what seemed hours in between the dreams, but when he'd drifted off again, they had come back instantly.

'Are you sick?' his mother said. 'You're all pale. Oh, Simon, you should have had your tea.'

He had stayed out for a long time the night before. For once he had kept a grudge against his mother, refused to be friends when he had come home, refused to eat.

'I couldn't sleep,' he said. 'I had bad dreams. Mum – can I stay off school?'

This was difficult. If he stayed off, she would have to stay off work and she could not afford it.

'You know I can't leave you on your own all day,' she said. 'What if Mrs Sampson found out?'

They had trouble with the neighbours sometimes. Mrs Sampson had called the welfare once, when Simon had been smaller, accusing Mrs Mason of neglect.

'She wouldn't,' pleaded Simon. 'Please, Mum. Just this once. I wouldn't move, I'll stay in bed all day.'

His mother became brisk. She laid her hand on his forehead, which was – unfortunately – quite cool.

'No. I'm sorry, love, I do sympathise, but there's too much at stake. If Mrs Sampson—'

'But she won't!'

'If she did. And there's another thing. We've had a teacher round already once this week, haven't we? I still don't know really why. What would happen if I let you off today? Another one might come. The truant officer. Simon – no!'

He had sat up in bed, supplicating her. But his mother's face was closed and he did not go on. He lay back slowly, rubbing his tired eyes.

'There's some kids . . .' he said.

She looked at him for quite some time, not speaking.

'Don't start that again,' she said, at last. She checked her watch.

'Simon. I've got to go to work. You've got to

81

go to school. I'll go and put your breakfast out. Get up.'

She turned away.

'I wish I hadn't told you lies,' said Simon, quietly. 'There *are* some kids. They're going to get me. I wish I hadn't told you all those things.'

His mother, almost through the door, turned and nodded.

'It's a pity, isn't it?' she said.

At the Royles' house, David was probably in a worse state even than Simon. He too had had a night of bad dreams, although his had been about punishment, and retribution. Asleep or awake, he had been obsessed with the idea that he was involved in something wrong, and that he would be found out very soon. Anna dragged him out of bed with none of the sympathy Simon's mum had shown, and gave him a stark warning.

'Listen, you little creep,' she said. 'If you think you're going to wriggle out of this, I'm telling you you're *dead wrong*. One word to anyone, one little whine to Mum – and you're finished, right? *Right?*'

David, in his pyjamas, nodded miserably. His sister was too big, too confident, too ruthless. He began to realise how Simon Mason must sometimes feel . . .

Downstairs at breakfast, Mrs Royle was quick to catch the mood. Almost before her son had picked up his spoon she was on to him.

'David? Are you all right, darling? You look . . . peculiar.'

Beside him, Anna gave off warnings. David kept his face down to his bowl, but a great wave of self-pity rose inside him. The cornflakes blurred as his eyes began to fill.

'Get on with you, Mum!' said Anna jokily. 'He's perfectly all right.'

'David?' repeated his mother.

'Yer,' he muttered. 'Fine. No, I'm fine, Mum. I couldn't . . . I couldn't get to sleep too well, that's all.'

'Oh dear, that's bad. Maybe you should take the morning off and get some sleep, then I can take you later?'

'Mum! That's ridiculous!' Anna crashed her spoon down, splashing milk across the tablecloth. Leaning across her brother to mop it up, she whispered 'No!' low and fiercely in his ear. The beginnings of a smile were wiped off his face.

'Anna, you're so clumsy,' said Mrs Royle. 'Why is that ridiculous? Surely a morning won't make any difference to his schooling?'

'Because it isn't tiredness,' said Anna. 'That's an excuse.'

It had been the only way, she thought. Much more kindness from his mum, and little David would have blurted out the lot. Their father had appeared in the doorway, doing up his tie. He was listening. Mother's face was grave.

'An excuse for what?' she asked. 'David?'

Still too soon to let him answer. Anna said impatiently: 'Oh, you know. That boy again. Simon Mason. He knocked his sandwiches on the grass. It wasn't serious, but David's such a wimp. Ask him.'

'I'd very much like to have the chance,' her mother said. 'Stop interrupting and let him speak.' Despite herself, she smiled. She thought that she had caught her daughter out. So Simon Mason was the name, was it? She would remember that. To her son she said: 'Is this true, dear? When did it happen?'

Their father had spun a chair round. He sat down on it, back to front, interested.

'It wasn't that bad,' muttered David, trying hard to guess what Anna wanted him to say. 'He ran into me at dinnertime, that's all. He sent me flying. I'm not a wimp.'

Anna was grinning. It was hardly World War II, was it? Her father winked at her.

'It could almost have been an accident from the sound of it,' he said.

'You keep out of this,' said Mrs Royle. 'You don't understand. He's done it once too often, this boy, he must be stopped. I'm going to ring them up.'

'Oh Mum!' went Anna, all exasperation. 'Don't you understand! If David calls his mother in to sort out Simple Simon, it will make it ten times worse. He'll get *really* bullied, not just messed about, he'll be a laughing stock to *everyone*. Leave us be, *please*, we'll sort it out.'

Mrs Royle looked at David, and David – torn horribly – backed his sister up. Mrs Royle made a hopeless gesture.

'Well,' smiled Mr Royle, pulling the chair from under him as he stood. 'To sum up, dear, I'd say you'd better take the kids' advice. Who'd be a judge, eh?'

He wandered out of the breakfast room, chuckling to himself. Anna came and touched her mother on the shoulder, lovingly.

'Please don't worry, Mum,' she said. 'It's only silly kids' stuff. He's just an idiot, is Simon. He's dead thick.'

'He's a spastic,' said David, bitterly.

And Mrs Royle turned on him, and told him off for using such 'cruel and stupid language', which made her feel a little better, but not much.

But at least I know his name, she thought, as she went to get her coat. That's something.

'What are you going to do?' asked Brian. He had waited on a corner this morning, in his tracksuit, until Louise had come along and picked him up in her car.

'What should I do?' replied Louise. 'Talk to him? Talk to them? Talk to Beryl Stacey? Cut my throat? I just don't really know.'

'She was very funny about the sandwiches, was Beryl,' said Brian. 'She went on as if Simon had done something really wrong. As if he'd tried to starve the Royle boy to death. Heaven knows what she'd have said if I'd told her about the rock!'

They were stopped at traffic lights. Louise reached across and touched Brian on the arm.

'Thank you for not,' she said. 'I don't think you'll regret it, though. I don't think he's a bad boy, really.'

'I think you're cracked,' said Brian.

But Mrs Stacey had something up her sleeve. She announced, before assembly began, that she had an important announcement to make later. Throughout the morning topic, and the prayer, and the notice-board, she sat solidly on her straight-backed chair, a fierce and solemn expression on her face. When everything else was over, she got to her feet and walked slowly to the lectern.

Although Mrs Stacey was quite small, she could be very frightening. She was broad and muscular, and heavy rather than fat. Her hair was tightly curled, and she kept the muscles in her face tight, also. In the long pause before she spoke, the children stirred uncomfortably.

'There are things going on in this school, children,' she said, 'that make me feel ashamed to be headteacher. There are things going on in this school that I would expect from nasty, uncaring, stupid children. There are things going on in this school that I will not tolerate.'

You could have heard a pin drop. None of the children so much as blinked, all eyes were glaring forward. On the platform, the teachers were equally still, their faces set and grim.

'Bullying,' said Mrs Stacey. 'That is the word I have been hearing. Acts of mindless violence, threats, petty, stupid vandalism. At first I would not credit it. I could not believe the word. Even now I am less than certain that it is going on here, in St Michael's School, in spite of our traditions. So I am giving you a warning, here, today, instead of any punishment.'

A low sigh, from many throats, rustled through the ranks of children. Good heavens, thought Louise, they can't *all* believe they're guilty, can they? Staring at the faces, though, it seemed they could. There was a smattering of tight, hard smiles now from the biggest boys, but only a smattering. Most of them were still in thrall, and crushed.

As the silence lengthened, Mrs Stacey glanced sideways at the rows of teachers on the platform, first left, then right, and Louise dropped her eyes. The head returned her gaze to the body of the hall, her round face rather smug. She could see the children suffering, digesting her warnings, fearing the worst, whatever that might be. She sought out Simon Mason and found him staring at her, his face rigid with expectation, as if any moment she was bound to call his name. Although he was only eight seats away, she did not notice David Royle, because he was hunched right forward, white with apprehension, unconsciously holding the front of his trousers with both hands. To David, the headteacher's words were like sharp arrows seeking out his heart, the secret of his shame. She would have been surprised.

'Good,' said Mrs Stacey. 'I think you understand me now. I am proud of this school, and I want you all to be. It is not a hard thing that I ask of you, it is a question, simply, as I have said before, of good behaviour and better manners – attitude. I have no intention of naming any names today, that is not my purpose. Those of you who are culprits know who you are, and you may be certain that I do, too. For the moment, I will tell you only this: anybody among you who wants to be a bully or a cheat – this is not the place for them. This is not the place and you will not be tolerated, whoever you may be. Is that understood?'

Nobody spoke – nobody knew they were expected to – and Mrs Stacey swelled up in front of them, like some awful, angry creature.

'Is that understood?' she bellowed. 'Answer me!'

There was a ragged chorus. It hardly raised the rafters, but it was loud enough. Mrs Stacey turned away and walked off the platform out of sight, leaving the ordinary teachers to take over. The children were subdued and quiet, and caused no trouble filing to their class-rooms.

'Well,' said Louise, sombrely to Brian. 'At least she didn't point out Simon as the murderer of poor Diggory. I thought she might have done. I'm going to have to talk to him, aren't I? Quick.'

'Yes,' Brian agreed. 'But what to say?'

It would not, Louise decided, be a very good idea to single Simon out in the circumstances, so she did not take him from any of his classes for their talk. But as soon as the buzzer went for break she left her office and went to the playground. She saw Simon, he saw her – and he began to run.

'Simon?' At first she did not call loudly, because she did not believe her eyes. Then he glanced over his shoulder, definitely and directly at her face, and went on running. She let out an impressive hoot: 'Simon! Simon Mason!'

Other children stopped their games and looked, but Simon disappeared behind the school. Miss Shaw, without another word, pushed back through the double doors, strode smartly across the width of the building, and emerged by the biology room. She was just in time to see him ducking round the corner ten metres away, heading straight for her. The shock on his face was comical.

'No!' she said, as he began to turn away. 'A game's a game, Simon, but if you run off now there will be trouble! Stand still!'

He stopped, gazing at the tarmac at his feet. As Louise approached she noticed how odd and pale he looked, how miserable. He had probably had enough of adults frightening him for one day, she thought.

'Simon,' she said, her voice much softer. 'I only want to talk to you. Things are getting out of hand, aren't they? I've had a chat with Mr Kershaw about yesterday. About David Royle and the sandwiches. We've got to do something.'

They were face to face. Simon did not reply, and Louise put a hand out to touch him. She was going to lift his chin. Simon flinched.

'Come on,' she said. 'I'm not going to punish you. I'm not going to rant and rave at you. Tell me about it. What happened with the sandwiches? And the rock?'

She dropped her hand and Simon, seeing this, raised his eyes, not quite up to hers. His face was tortured, as if he was fighting tears. He was, in fact, not sure exactly what he felt. He was in a turmoil. The kindness in her voice confused him most.

But in the end he did not respond to it. His fists clenched, his chin jerked sharply upwards, and he shouted into her startled face.

'What's the use of telling you? No one believes me anyway! What's the point?'

'Simon, Simon!' said Louise, but he was unstoppable. His face had reddened, his eyes were wide and wild.

'All the kids say I killed the gerbil, and Mrs

Stacey thinks so now! You heard her! She's going to expel me when I never did a thing! You pretend to believe me but you think I'm a liar, too! And that Mr Kershaw. I never chucked the rock, it was for self defence! They were going to smack me in!'

Even behind the school, Miss Shaw was acutely aware that they might be overheard. She did not want that, she wanted to protect this boy from himself. She made shushing sounds, she raised her hands to soften him, although she did not try to touch him this time.

'Well, never mind that now,' she said. 'Just calm down a bit. I don't believe you killed the gerbil, honestly. I—'

'But you don't believe that *they* did, do you? Now they're going to bash me up, aren't they? They had a trial!'

'A trial? Simon, please, stop this now! You're talking nonsense! No one's going to beat you up, you silly boy. Who do you think would do it, little David Royle?'

He looked into her face with withering scorn. But his shouting fit had passed. He shook his head.

'Not David Royle, Anna Royle. Anna and Rebekkah, who do you think? They bully me. They always bully me. I told you, didn't I?'

The buzzer sounded, and Louise let him go. Around the corner, Anna and Rebekkah just had time to corner him before the next lesson started, and demand to know where he had been the night before. It was a short and vicious meeting.

'We sentenced you,' said Anna. There was an

odd smile on her lips. 'We found you guilty and we chose a fitting punishment, and we're going to give it to you after school tonight, understood?'

Rebekkah also smiled.

'If you try to get away,' she said, 'it will be the worse for you, much worse. This time we've told our parents. About the rocks you chucked, and everything.'

'My dad's a lawyer,' Anna added. 'You know that, don't you? He says that you're in trouble, Simon. Deep, deep trouble.'

She pinched him, hard and painfully, to drive the message home.

Linda Mason, Simon's mother, rang the school at lunch-time to speak to Louise Shaw. She had thought about what she would say for ages, and had been worried that she would make herself look foolish. But Simon had said he was sick, Simon had not wanted to go to school, Simon had said there were some children out to 'get' him. What did it all add up to? Very little. But Miss Shaw had seemed a nice woman, sympathetic. Surely she would not mind a little chat about it? It was worth the risk.

Unfortunately, Mrs Stacey also wanted to talk to Louise Shaw, and Louise – knowing this – had left the school at the end of morning classes on the pretext that her car needed looking at. The secretary who answered the phone to Mrs Mason told her this, and asked if she could take a message. Mrs Mason, flustered, said not to bother, she would try later, maybe. It was not important.

She wondered for a few more minutes if she should walk up to St Michael's, to make sure that Simon was all right. But that was *really* silly, she decided, he would be furious. Still worrying, she put on the kettle for a cup of tea.

At afternoon break, Louise – quite deliberately – set out to corner David. He was not so fast as Simon, nor yet so canny. Until she had him trapped, he had not even realised that she was after him. She moved him gently round a corner near the rubbish skips, which were out of bounds. He looked longingly towards the noise of playing kids, then gave in. He still had no inkling that the next few minutes might be deadly difficult.

'Well, David. That was quite a talking to Mrs Stacey gave us this morning, wasn't it?'

He blinked. It was a typical teacher's question. What was he supposed to say?

'About bullying,' she continued. 'You've been bullied, haven't you? What do you think?'

The first flickers of panic began to gnaw at him. Had he been bullied? When? What was she referring to?

'It's okay,' he said.

'What! Being bullied! It's okay?'

'I don't mind,' he said. 'Not much. You know.'

He was mumbling, head well down. Anna would kill him when she knew he'd been talking to Loo-roll on his own. She'd told him not to, to avoid her like the plague.

Miss Shaw waited.

'You have been bullied, haven't you?' she asked. 'You do know what I'm talking about? David?'

She watched in fascination as a slow blush spread up his temples to his ears. He hunched his chin even deeper into his neck.

'Your sandwiches,' she said. 'Did they taste nice, all muddy? That was bullying, surely, wasn't it? That was the sort of thing Mrs Stacey had in mind. Or did you think she was on about the gerbil?'

Really, thought Louise, she should not be doing this. In its own way, this was bullying, as well. It would not have worked on Anna and Rebekkah because they would have known exactly how to handle it. She was picking on the weakest link.

'You went into the resources centre, didn't you?' she said abruptly. 'Were you with Anna and Rebekkah, or did you go alone?'

His head jerked up.

'No!'

His eyes were bright with terror. His teeth snapped shut on anything else he might let out. After a second or two, he shook his head.

'We never did,' he said. 'We never went in there. You ask Anna, Miss. You ask Rebekkah. It was Simon's fault, not ours, it was Simon. You ask Anna and Rebekkah.'

Louise could not go on. Whatever part poor

David might have played, he was not the culprit, anyone could see that. Oddly, he reminded her of Simon.

'Oh, run along now, David. Playtime will be over soon. Run along and meet your friends.'

He did not run, he walked. Another bit of fear and misery I've spread, thought Louise sadly. She, in her turn, needed to find a friend. Perhaps Brian would have a sensible opinion.

As it turned out, Louise did not speak to Brian until after she had made her mind up, and done what she had decided would be best. She had also had a brief confrontation with Mrs Stacey, which had been unpleasant. The headteacher had asked her coldly if she had come to terms yet with the fact that Simon Mason was a bully, and what punishment she had in mind for him. Louise had bitten her lip, and said the situation was at the forefront of her mind.

She went to the playing fields during the last part of the afternoon, tracking Brian down by the garish blueness of his tracksuit. Free from duty for the moment, he was doing kick-ups with a ball. He raised his eyebrows at her.

'Seventy-eight, seventy-nine, eighty!' He let the ball drop to the grass. 'I could have done a hundred if you hadn't interfered!'

'Oh shut up,' she said. 'This is serious.'

'Okay, if you say so. Look, I've got to go and make some phone calls in a minute, I was putting it off.'

Louise blew air between her lips.

'I've just made one,' she said. 'I've got a parent coming after school. A steaming one.'

'Mrs Mason?'

'Worse. Anna and David Royle's mother. She'll probably bring Rebekkah Tanner's, too. And a lawyer, from the way she went on on the phone.'

Brian picked the ball up in one large hand, and tucked it underneath his arm. He began to walk towards the school.

'Sounds bad. Why did she phone you? Have the kids been complaining about dear Simon?'

'You don't listen. I phoned her, I said. I phoned her about bullying. I said it was notoriously difficult to pin down, but I was concerned about something that was happening.'

'Hold on. What are you suggesting? Surely not her two precious kids . . .? Phew!'

Louise kicked a clod of earth, spattering mud on her shoe and tights.

'I didn't get the chance. She didn't exactly hit the roof, but her voice was like acid. She said she knew all about the bullying, and that it had gone much too far already. Her children had begged her not to make a fuss about it, they'd been absolutely noble. Those were her actual words. But she was their mother, and it was time to override them. She's coming after school. As close to four o'clock as she can make it.'

They had reached the edge of the grass, and stopped for a moment before stepping on to the tarmac.

'Oh well,' said Brian. 'Is it such a bad thing, in the end? If she hadn't decided to do something concrete Beryl Stacey would have done quite soon, I guess. And like it or not, if little Simon keeps using stones and things . . . Louise, it could end up very serious.'

'It's not him,' she replied. 'I've spoken to him, Brian, and I've spoken to David Royle. You can mock me if you like, but I'm certain. They killed the gerbil, too. The Royles and Rebekkah. At least, they left the cover off the tank.'

'Ouch,' said Brian. 'And Mrs Royle's on her way, is she? To hear you say that. Ouch.'

'You don't believe me, do you?'

He bounced the ball, once, on the hard surface of the playground.

'I'm not the problem, am I?' he said. 'Have you got proof?'

'No,' said Louise Shaw.

CHAPTER THIRTEEN

Anna and Rebekkah had been caught out by Simon's disappearing act before, and this time they were determined he would not get away with it. In the last five minutes of their last lesson they were bouncing up and down like yo-yos, looking through the windows, whispering to each other, exchanging anguished glances. Their teacher, Mr Bailey, told them off once or twice but not with any anger. In his eyes, Anna Royle could do no wrong.

When the buzzer clicked, then settled down to a sustained rasping, they shot out of their desks like rubber balls. Anna barged into another girl and knocked some books on to the floor.

'Anna,' said Mr Bailey. 'Slow down. What's got into you?'

'Sorry, sir! Please, can we go, sir! It's very important, honestly!'

She was not waiting for consent. She was edging for the front, pushing subtly, clawing people from her path.

'Oh, go on, the pair of you,' the teacher said.

'You're more like Visigoths than girls. Mind out, Danielle, you'll be crushed to death!'

They burst through the class-room door like bullets from a machine-gun. But quick though they had been, some children had been quicker. The corridor was filling up, the noise of chattering was rising. Anna and Rebekkah ran, but they had to put their heads down and do some solid pushing to get through. And the small kids' door, which Simon would have to use, was right down the other end.

'Damn!' panted Anna. 'He'll get away. Shift! You! Get out of it, can't you!'

Rebekkah, beside her in the milling crowd, shoved a girl violently aside.

'He'll wait!' she said. 'He wouldn't dare to run away, not after yesterday. He knows we'll murder him!'

But Simon had not waited, nor was he waiting now. At the first click of the buzzer outside Mrs Earnshaw's room, he had careered to the front. Mrs Earnshaw, who had still been teaching, had gasped in astonishment.

'Simon!'

'Stop him!' squeaked David Royle.

'Oyoyoyoyoy!' roared almost everybody else.

Simon knew he was in trouble, and he also knew which sort he feared the most. Mrs Earnshaw might shout at him in the morning, Mrs Stacey might threaten him with all kinds of things, but neither of them would lay a finger on him. Anna Royle would, she'd smash his nose in, given half a chance. He wasn't going to let her try, he couldn't bear to. He ran.

Before he reached the door, David reared up before him, a look of martyred anguish on his face. He had to stop Simon, but knew he did not have the courage to do it properly. Simon, as he thundered past, recognised his fear. She's told him not to let me escape, he thought – and he has. She'll batter him as well, her own brother!

'Simon!' repeated Mrs Earnshaw. 'Don't you dare!'

Simon dared. He jerked the door open without another backward glance.

'Oh, *Miss*!' he heard David wail.

He went.

The corridor at their end of the school was empty still, so Simon made it to the exit in record time. He stared out across the playground and the playing fields, but saw no one close enough to threaten him. Before even his own class could get into the corridor he was through the swing doors and away. Three hundred metres or so to the main gate; then – he hoped – he would be safe.

He was about half-way when Anna and Rebekkah got clear into the yard and spotted him. For the moment they were both dismayed. He had his head down and he was moving very fast, like a small train. But they paused only for an instant, and their speed when they moved forward was increased by anger. Both of them, oddly, felt he had no right to run away from them at all.

There were spectators now. The children Anna

and her friend had barged through knew that something must be going on, and they did not want to miss it. As the girls hared across the empty playing field they streamed after them, shouting. It was the noise that attracted the attention of some teachers, Louise among them. She glanced through her office window, saw the girls and their followers, and was just in time to spot a little boy running through the gates on to the road. A little boy who could only be Simon Mason . . .

Brian saw it too, from his position on the far side of the playing fields. A chase, a hunt, a long straggle of children spreading from the main school building. He blew a final whistle and waved the teams towards the changing rooms, then began to jog towards the action. He was still too far to work out who was chasing whom.

Anna and Rebekkah heard Miss Shaw shouting at them – she had a most distinctive hoot. Naturally, they ignored her, although Rebekkah did glance backwards. The deputy head was standing outside the double doors, legs apart, hand upraised. Some of the followers nearest her dropped out of the race.

'Come on!' yelled Anna, who had reached the gate. 'We'll say we didn't hear her. We're out of earshot! Where is he? There he is!'

Simon, unluckily, was still visible to them – just. Even as Anna pointed, he turned sharp right off the main road and disappeared. Another half a second and they would have missed him.

'Where's he gone?' said Rebekkah.

She knew, they both did. The hill rose steeply to their right, above the trees and houses.

'Chalkpit,' said Anna, grimly. 'He's always in there, isn't he? He was probably in there when we had that stupid trial.'

'Crikey,' said Rebekkah, 'I never thought of that. You wouldn't think he'd have the guts, would you?'

Although the chalkpit was a completely forbidden place, both of them had been in before, of course. At one time or another almost all the children of St Michael's had risked it, usually to show how brave they were. It had been disused for several years, and the fences, and even the big front gates, had rotted slowly. According to tradition, some boys had been killed there once while bird-nesting, and Mrs Stacey issued grim warnings from time to time about dangerous tunnels and rusty old machinery. If anyone was caught trespassing, she said, the consequences would be dire.

Simon, who had long ago forgotten any fears about the place, was confident that Anna and Rebekkah would not follow him, even if they guessed he'd gone to ground. He wriggled in through his favourite hole and gazed at the high, white blank of the chalkface with a powerful feeling of relief. It was quiet, apart from the screaming of gulls, and it had an air of peacefulness that he loved. Slowly, the panic drained away from him.

But he was not fool enough to stay out in the open, for all that. He got his breath back a little, then ducked behind a low piece of broken wall from where he could watch the gates and access road. It was with utter shock that he saw Anna and Rebekkah turn the corner and run – without the slightest hesitation – straight for the quarry entrance. For a moment he was frozen, then he turned and fled. He realised suddenly what he had done. He was in a lonely, isolated place, no one to help at all. If they caught him, he was done for.

At the gateway, the girls had stopped. To them, the chalkpit was not a place of peace and refuge, it was a dump. The bricks of the buildings were a dirty white from years of chalk-dust, with rusty stains all over them. There was a crane half on its side, its broken jib bent grotesquely across a railway truck. Between piles of rubble, scrubby grass grew in clumps. And going in spelled trouble.

'Come on,' said Rebekkah, who was feeling uncertain. 'It's not worth it, is it? We don't even know if he went in there. Let's go.'

Anna was scornful.

'Where else did he get to? You're chicken. No one's going to find us, are they?'

'Where's David?' asked Rebekkah illogically. 'Didn't we ought to wait for him?'

Anna ignored that. She shook the gates until rust fell.

'Look,' she said. 'That chain's completely

rotten. One good push and it would just give way.'

'Don't! That's trespassing! Oh Anna, don't do that!'

But Anna did, and the big gates parted squeakily. She seized her friend by the sleeve and hauled her through.

'You go that way, I'll go over here! Look in all the sheds and things, he hasn't had time to find a proper place. See that big iron thing up there? We'll meet by that if we don't find him.'

Rebekkah might have protested, but she did not get the chance. Anna ran off behind a spoil-heap of chalk, eager as a terrier. She paused for just a moment, then set off in her turn. Secretly, she rather hoped they would not find him. She smelled big trouble. Being best friends with Anna Royle, just sometimes, could be—

Then there was a shriek, and Rebekkah's heart began to pound. It was Anna's voice, alive with triumph.

'Over here! Over here! Rebekkah!'

Her doubts forgotten, Rebekkah rushed towards the sound. Anna was on top of a pile of junk, pointing. About a hundred metres away, close under the vertical chalkface, was an old black metal structure, a gantry of some kind. Half-way up it, in full view, clung Simon.

'Got him!' yelled Anna. 'Trapped like a rat! What a fool, what a total, raving idiot!'

'Like a monkey up a pole!' Rebekkah shouted.

'You're too clumsy for a monkey, Simple Simon! You're going to fall and break your neck!'

As she shouted, Simon began to slip.

Back at the school, David had watched the pursuit of first Simon, then his sister and Rebekkah with growing worry. At first he had decided to stay inside, but a mass of pushing children had thrust him out into the yard. He had seen Miss Shaw set off, bellowing, he had seen Mrs Stacey come running out and talk to several other teachers. He had not seen Mr Kershaw, though, who was winging in from a different direction.

'It's your sister!' someone told him, with excitement. 'She's going to get that Simon Mason! Aren't you going to help?'

That was the problem. He did not want to, but he had to. Bad enough that he'd let Simon get away, there would be retribution for that, in plenty. But if he failed to turn up for the kill . . . The trouble was, the teachers. They were everywhere, trying to bring some order to the chaos, arguing and shouting at the kids. He'd have no chance running for the gate.

It occurred to David that if he did a wide detour, if he struck out away from the body of the crowd, he might make it to a smaller gateway along the wire fence. He might not even be noticed, if he was lucky. Because fear grew instantly, he began to move. He would not give himself time to change his mind.

He did quite well at first. No one seemed to

notice him as he sneaked around a corner, no one yelled as he began to run. After about a hundred metres he felt a lift of exhilaration, and glanced back over his shoulder. There was no pursuit.

Then ahead of him, he saw Mr Kershaw's tracksuit, violent, garish blue. He was running on a long diagonal, apparently to join Miss Shaw at the main gate. But as David spotted him he spotted David, and changed course slightly. David changed his own direction, to get clear, and the sports teacher curved round some more, to head him off. David, a lump of cold lead in his stomach, stopped altogether. He turned, as if to run the other way, then looked back. Mr Kershaw, fit and fast, bore down on him. David noticed how his trainers threw up small lumps of earth with the power in his legs.

'David!' Mr Kershaw's voice was very sharp. He was not even panting. 'Just where do you think you're going to? What's going on?'

It all came over him in a mighty rush. What little control he had was swamped entirely. He did not see his mother's Volvo estate draw up outside the gates, he did not see Mrs Royle and Avril Tanner get out and slam the doors. His eyes were blurred, his shoulders shaking hopelessly.

He was dissolving into tears.

CHAPTER FOURTEEN

Simon had hurt himself in the fall. He had dropped perhaps a metre, from one metal girder to another one below, landing with the iron bar across his stomach. It had winded him, and given him a sharp pain in his lower ribs, but the softness of his belly had saved him from breaking any bones. He felt like a piece of wet washing, hanging from a line four metres from the ground. But although his eyes were misty with pain, the criss-crossed girders he had clambered up still looked sharp and deadly between him and the earth. To the girls, he looked like easy meat.

'You might as well come down,' called Anna, even before they had reached the bottom of the gantry. 'You might as well come and take your medicine. Ah, is diddums all right, then? Look, diddums is crying!'

Rebekkah giggled.

'Shall I climb up with a hankie, diddums? Shall I come and wipe your lickle nosey-wosey?'

In fact, Simon wiped his own tears away, rubbing one hand across his face while holding on with the other. The wiping hand was sticky, covered in tar and oil. His clothes were, too. Everything was ruined. A wave of hatred gripped him for these girls.

They were at the bottom, looking up. Anna had seen the filthy state that he was in, and gingerly touched the metal girders.

'Come down now,' she ordered, rather as a teacher might have done. 'If we have to come up after you, it'll be much worse, I promise you.'

Simon put both hands on the horizontal bar and pulled himself up on to it, balancing on one knee. He swayed, but managed to grab an upright and steady himself. He studied the spot that he had slipped from. Two metres beyond it was the platform he had been aiming for. Unlike the girls, he knew the place. He knew escape routes.

Without speaking, he started to clamber up again, with a speed that surprised them. He climbed fast and well, not at all like the clumsy lump they took him for. They began to shout at him.

'Come down! You'll slip! You'll never get away with it!'

When Simon reached the platform, he paused to catch his breath. He glanced down at the upturned faces, wishing he had a rock to drop, or a bowl of boiling oil. But he was safe, at least – they'd never try to follow him.

'Okay!' said Anna. 'If that's the way you want it, mate! We're coming after you!'

'Anna!' said Rebekkah, in distress. 'We'll get dirty!'

Anna said something short and rude, with an expression that could have killed. She launched herself at the bottom girders, searching for the best hand and footholds. Rebekkah stepped backwards, feeling foolish.

'Oh!' she squeaked. 'Anna, it's too late! He's—'

Anna jumped back to join her, cursing. Simon had left the platform and was standing on a narrow iron bar that stretched from the gantry into the chalkface. It did not look thick enough to support a lot of weight.

'He's going to do a high-wire act! He's going to fall!'

'You idiot!' yelled Anna.

Simon gave himself no time to think. He had often wondered if you could get across the tie-rod, which led to one of the narrow tracks that ran along the chalk cliff for the workmen; but balancing was hardly one of his great skills, even on the ground. Then he was on it, staggering across one foot after the other, arms out from his sides, a demented puppet. He was on the path, face pressed into the rough chalk, heart pounding violently with shock.

And triumph! He had done it! He had done something impossible!

He turned carefully around, pressing his back now into the lumpy chalk, a warm breeze on his face. He could see across the town, he could see the harbour, the sea beyond, the boats and ships. He looked downwards and his stomach lurched, it seemed so far. The ledge was narrow, and all at once the chalk behind him began to press into his back, as if it was trying to push him off, to make him tumble down the cliff to where the girls were staring up at him, still silenced by his act.

To left and right the path stretched along the cliff face, narrow, crumbling, unfenced.

The sense of triumph drained rapidly away.

Mrs Royle came through the school gates ready for a fight, and when she saw her little boy in tears she turned into a fury.

'Over there!' she told Mrs Tanner. 'I don't believe it, Avril! What's that man doing to him?'

Mrs Tanner glanced at David, then searched the crowd nearer the school buildings for her daughter. It was confusion, a pell-mell mass of children and teachers, with the small, squat form of Mrs Stacey apparently haranguing all of them.

'Where's Rebekkah? I can't see her or Anna anywhere.'

Mrs Royle was not listening. She was storming across the grass towards her son. Mr Kershaw saw her coming and touched David's shoulder.

'It's your mum. For heaven's sake dry your eyes.'

David looked up, and howled even more.

'Mum!' he wailed. 'Mum!'

'David! What are they doing to you?'

Mr Kershaw was acutely uncomfortable. He could see Beryl Stacey waving her arms about, herding the children back into school to get their coats, dispersing them. Louise had left the gate and was striding fast towards him. Mrs Royle, David hugged tightly to her side, angrily turned to face her.

'Miss Shaw! What is happening in this place? It's like a madhouse and my child's in tears! Who's responsible?'

Louise, close to, looked strained.

'Good afternoon, Mrs Royle,' she began.

'Nonsense!' retorted Mrs Royle crisply. 'Where is my daughter? Why is my son crying? David, who was it bullying you this time? Was it that boy again?'

'Oh, come on!' said Louise, sharply.

'*Please*,' said Mr Kershaw.

Mrs Tanner had arrived. Now Mrs Stacey was following, having left the ordering of the children to the other teachers.

'Ladies,' said Brian. 'Calm down. This is serious.'

'Where's Rebekkah?' demanded Avril Tanner aggressively. 'Where's the little bully?'

'Look!' Louise exploded. 'When I rang you, Mrs Royle, I told you there were doubts! Will you kindly stop making accusations!'

'Hah!' hissed Mrs Royle. 'Are you going to deny the evidence of your own eyes? David's crying! Are you going to deny that Simon Mason is involved?'

Mrs Stacey, her face a mixture of anger and curiosity, came panting up.

111

'Will somebody explain?' she said. 'Miss Shaw, remember your position! Losing one's temper is not professional!'

Louise had bright red spots high on her cheeks, but she controlled herself.

'I'm sorry, Mrs Stacey. I'm sorry, Mrs Royle. But please understand, the situation is not as simple as it seems. Simon Mason—'

Mrs Stacey interrupted.

'Is he involved? Where is he, then? Who precisely ran out through those gates? I saw Anna and Rebekkah.'

'Run out!' said Mrs Royle, horrified. 'What, into the road?!'

'She was running after Simon,' said Louise. 'She was chasing him. As was your daughter, Mrs Tanner.'

'Rebekkah? But why?'

'Because he's been making their lives a misery, I expect!' said Mrs Royle furiously. 'Because he's been picking on David! Why are you crying? Is it because of Simon Mason?'

David burst into renewed sobs, and Mrs Royle hugged him to her stomach. Brian was acutely embarrassed now, while Mrs Stacey had gone white with suppressed anger. To have such a scene in public was appalling to her. Despite the best efforts of the other teachers, children were still rubbernecking eagerly.

'That is enough!' she snapped. 'I will not have public brawling on my precincts. Miss Shaw – briefly – tell me what has happened. No, Mrs

Royle, please let her speak! You may have your say afterwards.'

Louise controlled her breathing with difficulty. She had never known such dislike for anyone as she felt for Mrs Royle now. She cleared her throat.

'As I understand it,' she began, 'there was something in the air at break this morning. I spoke to Simon Mason and he said he was afraid. He told me that he had been threatened with a beating-up. By Anna and Rebekkah.'

For a short while there was pandemonium. Mrs Royle and Mrs Tanner both started shouting at full pitch. Amid the jumbled accusations and denials, the word 'liar' could be heard. Louise, pale and determined, did not respond to any of it.

Mrs Stacey had had her hand up for many seconds before the noise subsided. When there was quiet, she said: 'Did you believe him, Louise? Simon Mason has been known to lie before.'

'He's a known liar and a known bully!' said Mrs Royle. 'My children have already told me what he's been up to! They said he'd make these accusations! But you believe *him*, do you, Miss Shaw? You'd rather believe a known liar than our children?'

Louise's voice was low.

'I don't know really what I believe,' she said. 'The whole business is horrible. But I saw Simon chased out of this school by Anna and Rebekkah and I don't know why. I don't believe it's just a case of simple bullying by one boy.'

'When I asked David,' put in Brian rapidly, 'he burst into tears. If that means anything.'

'It means he's terrified!' yelled his mother. 'The whole thing's out of all control! I had to drag the name of Simon Mason out of them almost by force! They were protecting him! And now you take his part! That's why David's crying, you great stupid man! *Anyone* would cry!'

It was at this point that Linda Mason was noticed. She had walked through the main gate and looked around, and seen the group of people on the playing field. As she got within earshot, fear grew inside her. Louise saw her and jumped slightly, touching Mrs Stacey and indicating with her head. The two angry mothers looked as well. Although they did not know her, they said no more.

'Mrs Mason,' said Louise faintly.

'I thought I'd better come,' she said. 'There's something going on, something's happening to Simon. I thought I'd better get to the bottom of it.'

Mrs Stacey coughed into her hand.

'Yes,' she replied. 'I think perhaps you're right. These ladies . . .'

Linda Mason interrupted.

'But where is he?' She looked from face to face, and the truth fell in on her.

'Doesn't anybody know?'

At the chalkpit, Rebekkah thought – quite happily – that Simon had won. It seemed the best way out for all of them.

'We'd better leave him now,' she suggested, in a rather plaintive voice. 'There's no way we can get to him up there, no way. Someone'll be coming soon.'

Anna did not reply at once. She was gazing up at what she could see of Simon, high above her on the ledge. He still had his back pressed to the chalk, so not much of him was visible.

'Why?' she asked. 'Why should anyone come, no one knows we're here. Where do you think he's going to go, Rebekkah? Grow wings and fly away? Unless he stays up there all night we'll get him, won't we?'

Rebekkah had an uncomfortable suspicion that her friend might be prepared to wait not just all night but all week too, if necessary. For herself, she'd had enough.

'Oh come on,' she said. 'It's boring waiting. We've scared him half to death and wrecked his clothes, isn't that enough? You can have another go tomorrow, if you want.'

At that moment Simon moved. They knew it, because a small amount of broken chalk slid off the ledge and skittered down towards them. Anna pondered.

'If we could make him shift,' she said, 'he might even fall. That would be good, wouldn't it?'

'Shut up, Anna! You're ridiculous.'

The fall of chalk had frightened Simon, but he got over it. The ledge, or pathway, was riddled with soft, dangerous patches, but he knew he could avoid them. If he followed the chalkface round he'd come to broader paths that led eventually to safer places to get down. Places to wait, as well, until the girls had gone away.

His mouth was dry for the first few steps. The track was only half a metre wide, and lumps of chalk stuck out at shoulder height, causing him to crouch. Looking down after a minute, he saw the ruined roofs of quarry buildings and the cluttered paths between them, but could no longer see the girls. He stopped, hoping to hear them. He heard the wind, some traffic in the distance, crying seagulls.

I wonder what I look like from a distance, Simon thought. He pictured the chalkface, like a great blank white wall carved out of the hill. He would be a black dot crawling on it. A fly on a big blancmange.

He began to feel better. Ahead of him the path split into two, one branch leading horizontally, the other curving upwards. The upwards path

116

was wider, safer-looking. He would take the upward path. He heard a clanking from below, as if the girls had pushed over an oil-drum, and he wondered if they might be giving up. But still they were not visible. Let's keep it that way, eh, he told himself. Let's make them think I've vanished into thin air . . .

Below, to Rebekkah's acute discomfort, Anna was collecting things to throw. She had seen some handy lumps of iron – as big as a fist, cut off from some old welding, by the look of it – and had pulled aside some sheets of tin to get at them. There were some jagged flints, as well, that she pointed out to her friend.

'Come on,' she said. 'Don't hang about. He'll show up in a minute, and we'll get him. You're not chicken, are you?'

Rebekkah was. She was horrified.

'No,' she said.

Mrs Mason was having no more nonsense. When Mrs Royle started making accusations, she just shouted.

'Where is he? My little boy? I don't care what anybody's done, I want to know he's safe!'

Mrs Royle looked uncomfortable, but Mrs Stacey seemed to understand. She got very brisk and businesslike.

'You're right,' she said. 'Mrs Royle, Mrs Tanner, if there is to be an argument we'll have it later, if you please. Louise, do you have any idea where these children might have gone? Anybody?'

Nobody did. They were an odd, embarrassed lot, not wanting to look at each other's faces.

'David?' said Louise. Mrs Royle reddened.

'I don't see why—' But Brian interrupted her.

'He cried,' he said. 'Didn't you, David? You cried when I stopped you. Why?'

Before his mother could intervene again, David was in floods of tears. It was mainly incoherent, but the word chalkpit could be discerned. Not just once, but three times.

'Simon plays in the chalkpit?' asked Mrs Stacey. 'Are you certain, dear? Surely *none* of my children . . .'

You sound just like Mrs Royle, thought Louise. Surely none of *her* children are bullies. Not much!

'Have you been there?' asked Louise. 'David? Have you been there? And Anna?'

He sobbed harder. They had not, he insisted, not ever. But yesterday, while they'd waited . . . Simon Mason . . . He thought maybe . . .

'That's enough!' cried Mrs Royle. 'He's upset! David, darling, don't say any more.'

'We've got to go!' said Mrs Mason. 'Now!'

Mr Kershaw added quietly: 'I'm going to call an ambulance. Just in case.'

'No!' said Mrs Tanner. 'No!'

But Brian was already on his way to the school building. The others, with David jerking from his mother's hand, began to make raggedly for the gate. Mrs Mason was soon out in front, half walking, half running, with Louise trying to catch up.

'My car!' called Mrs Royle. 'We could go in my car! David! You must get in the car, you mustn't watch in case there's . . .'

'Shut up!' screamed Simon Mason's mother.

He had crept about two hundred metres before they spotted him again. The going had been easier up the broad new path, and Simon had not had to press himself against the chalk. At one point he had found a good deep dip in which he could have hidden if he had wanted. In fact, he had lain down in the sun, out of the wind, and been very comfortable for a minute or two. But the worry had forced him onwards. He could not stay up there all evening, and he wanted to get near the place from where he could get down. In his heart of hearts, he hoped and thought the girls would give up pretty quickly, and go away.

There had been one very bad bit, where the surface of the path had turned to a loose, crumbly texture. As he had put his feet on it, the lumps of chalk had rolled underneath them, turned to dust. The edge of the pathway had been soft, unstable, dangerous. Over it, the drop was enormous, higher than a house.

Past this part, Simon relaxed a little. Another hundred metres, and he would be in an area of paths he knew quite well, although there was some more crumbly stuff to come. He stopped every few steps, sometimes dropping down and creeping to the very edge to peep over past the clumps of wiry grass. He saw movements between the old buildings, shadows and waving bushes, but no girls. He began to dare to hope that they had gone.

But they had not. They had lost sight of him for some minutes, but Anna hardly cared. She had collected lumps of metal, made Rebekkah pick up flints, and organised the carrying of them through the quarry yard. Rebekkah – by accident or design – had dropped hers several times, but Anna had just laughed at her. She was feeling good, really excited, and there was stuff for throwing all around them, however hard Rebekkah seemed to wish there wasn't. When she judged they had moved along the chalkface far enough, she looked out from behind a ruined wall.

'There he is,' she said. 'See up there, a sitting duck. He's groping his way along like an old blind man. Come on – let's go in for the kill!'

She ran, and as she ran she whooped. Simon heard her, froze, and turned his head to gaze out across the quarry. He did, indeed, have his hands stretched out in front of him, one foot was poised, not yet fully on the ground. He was at a bad bit, the last bad bit, and he had been shuffling along infinitely slowly, his tongue gripped between his lips in concentration.

He heard and saw her and felt sick. She was coming fast, with Rebekkah following much more slowly. When she was close, Anna selected a jagged lump of steel and pulled her arm back in a throwing stance.

'No!' he shouted. 'Don't chuck it!'

He saw the rusty lump fly up, turning in the sun. It thudded into the cliff beneath him, more than a metre under where he stood. He squeaked in fright, and Anna ran in closer.

'*Chuck*, Rebekkah!' she shouted over her shoulder. '*Get* the little toad!'

As the next chunk came winging up, Simon moved backwards to avoid it. Even so, it missed by only centimetres, less than arm's length. It cracked into the rock in front of him, raising a cloud of dust and earth. He could no longer shout. He was choked with fear.

Anna was close. He could see into her open mouth as she yelled. He saw the muscles in her bare arm twang. He jumped forward, trying to anticipate the shot. He changed his mind, jumped back the way he'd come. He turned quickly on the narrow path, turned to run away. He felt the chalk beneath his feet collapse, heard slipping rock, heard his own scream. He had the impression of Anna's face also turning to a scream. He had a vision of an avalanche he'd seen on some film once; he slipped sideways and downwards into a sliding mass of chunks of chalky rock.

Rebekkah, from ten metres, saw Simon come sliding down the chalkface at appalling speed, any sound he might be making lost in the terrific roar. She saw Anna, faced with the avalanche, jump backwards like a coiled spring. A cloud of white dust burst upwards from Simon's landing and rolled over her in weird slow-motion. When

121

Rebekkah reached her, her hair was full of chalk, she was like a circus clown.

But now no one was laughing.

CHAPTER SIXTEEN

For a few moments, as the dust began to settle, there was silence in the quarry yard. Anna stared at Rebekkah, her face blank with fright. Rebekkah stared past her friend, at the pile of earth and rock which marked the bottom of the chalkface. If Simon was alive, he made no noise. If he was badly injured, there were no screams or moans.

'Rebekkah,' said Anna quietly. 'We've got to run.'

'No!' cried Rebekkah. They were both startled by the force of it. 'He might be hurt!'

Anna did not argue, it was as though she had not thought of that possibility. She turned to look, then both girls began to walk back to the cliff. They could see him now, lying like a broken toy, his arms and legs at dreadful angles. He was covered in thick dust, everything about him white. It was horrible, as if he were some sort of instant ghost.

A noise escaped from Anna's throat, like a sob.

'Don't touch him!'

The shout was so completely unexpected that both girls jumped. Their heads snapped backwards and they saw people running. Miss Shaw, another woman, and their mothers. In the rear, but coming very fast, the unmistakeable blue tracksuit of Mr Kershaw.

The girls were close, they had been about to bend to Simon. Under the white mask they saw blue bruising and red blood. His eyes were closed. They held themselves rigid, straight and nervous. Anna could not help noticing that one of his arms, at least, was broken. She felt sick.

The woman who must be Simon's mother reached him a half a step before Miss Shaw, and Anna had never seen anything remotely like the expression of pain and terror on her face. She herself felt an emotion that she knew was guilt or shame, although it flooded her too quickly for coherent thought. She stumbled backwards from Simon and his mother's face, but caught Rebekkah's eye. They stared at each other for a moment, their skin so white it was almost transparent. They understood at last what they had done.

'Don't move him!' said Louise urgently. She was talking to Mrs Mason this time, touching her, gently restraining her. 'Don't even lift anything off him. The ambulance will be here soon. You must leave it to the experts, in case his back's hurt.'

Mrs Mason began to cry as Brian came up. Mr Kershaw looked curiously at the girls, then knelt beside the unconscious boy. Mrs Royle and Mrs Tanner, strangely uncomfortable in the company of Mrs Stacey, stood beside a shed, not coming closer. But they wanted to talk to their daughters, obviously. Mrs Royle finally made an urgent gesture with her hand.

'The ambulance is on its way,' said Mr Kershaw. 'He'll be all right soon, Mrs Mason. He'll be in expert hands.'

Mrs Royle gestured once more, this time angrily. Anna and Rebekkah moved towards the women. Anna noticed her brother hiding behind a quarry building, and guessed he'd been told to keep away. Faintly, an ambulance siren came to her ears.

'It's coming!' said Rebekkah. 'I can hear an ambulance!'

'Anna,' said her mother. 'What has been going on?'

Anna opened her mouth to lie, but nothing would come out.

'Has he fallen?' said Mrs Tanner, unnecessarily. 'Were you going to help him?'

There were many eyes on them. Their mothers', the headteacher's, even David's. Louise and Brian had turned back to look. Only Mrs Mason took no notice. The ambulance siren was getting quickly louder.

'Yes,' said Anna. 'We were . . .'

'We were chasing him,' said Rebekkah. 'Anna threw some chunks of iron.'

There was a choking silence. Then the squeal

of brakes, followed by a metallic rattling of the quarry gates. The siren was switched off.

'Is that true?' asked Mrs Royle.

'Yes,' said Anna. 'I'm sorry, Mum. It is.'

It was the grown-ups who were probably most confused. Mrs Stacey and Mrs Royle and Mrs Tanner. There were parts of it that Louise and Brian did not understand, but most of those they thought they'd work out soon enough. Simon's mother thought she understood it perfectly, but some of it she did not want to put into words. Simon had been picked on by three cruel and vicious children – but then, he seemed to ask for it, somehow. This was her deepest, and most secret worry.

The headteacher seemed to have most trouble in accepting the known facts. Despite the girls' confessions, she was insistent even at the quarry – after Simon had been taken off to hospital – that nothing hasty must be done. Mrs Royle and Mrs Tanner were urged to take the children home 'away from any more upset' – and well away, in fact, from further awkward questions. Mrs Mason, naturally, went in the ambulance.

'I'd never have believed it,' said Mrs Stacey, as the teachers walked back to the school. 'I'm sure there'll be a simple explanation, aren't you, Louise?'

'I don't know,' said Louise. 'I think we'd better see what emerges, don't you? I doubt if we'll know the truth immediately.'

'I doubt if we'll know the truth at all,' Brian put in. 'But at the moment, we don't even know if he's badly hurt.'

Mrs Stacey was certain that he wouldn't be. She said it with pathetic hope, but fortunately, she was right. Simon had a broken arm, a broken ankle, and cuts and bruises and abrasions. With that weight taken off her, the headteacher was able to think about the implications for the school. Louise, at first, was roped in as her ally.

'We must stamp it out, of course,' said Mrs Stacey, when they talked. 'The Royle children and Rebekkah are very good examples, really, because they're so *unexpected*. I mean, normally with bullying, it's a different . . . *type*. Perhaps I'll do a talk about it in assembly. What do you think?'

Despite the nonsense about what 'type' of children did bullying, Louise was pleasantly surprised that Mrs Stacey was prepared to make an issue of it. She'd been afraid that the whole thing would have been brushed under the carpet.

'It's a good idea,' she replied. 'But you'd better pick your words, Anna's father is a lawyer, isn't he? We don't want any libel actions.'

It was a joke, but Mrs Stacey was quite frightened by it. And later, she drew Louise aside to tell her that she'd had a call from Mrs Royle. Her children, she had said, were deeply upset about the affair and would not be coming in for a few days; neither would Rebekkah.

'That's quite wise,' Louise responded. She

caught Mrs Stacey's expression. 'Oh. There's more?'

'There is. She says she's heard the details now, and is most concerned. She says Simon Mason has been bullying them repeatedly, blackening their names with accusations, and has threatened David with some sort of martial arts weapon in the past. She says she and her husband are by no means sure that they had anything to confess to.'

'Not even throwing things at a defenceless boy!' Louise said, heatedly. 'Not even knocking him off a cliff! That's marvellous, isn't it? That's truly marvellous.'

Mrs Stacey let the sarcasm go. Her eyes had become shrewd.

'Weapons, Louise. Do you know anything about a weapon?'

Louise remembered the kubutan, but dismissed it. Even Brian had let that silly subject drop.

'No,' she said, 'I don't. But I do know I suspected those kids of terrorising Simon, and I do know I heard Anna and Rebekkah admit they'd done it. Ask Mr and Mrs Royle if they think a broken ankle's anything to confess to!'

'Don't get heated, dear,' said Mrs Stacey, mildly. 'It's the truth we're seeking, not . . . Well, let's avoid emotional responses, shall we? Sadly, it is the truth that Simon can't be trusted, isn't it? Even his mother admits that he tells lies.'

'In this case, he was a clear-cut victim,' said Louise. 'In this case, there is no doubt.'

Mrs Stacey's eyes held hers steadily.

'Life's rarely like that, dear,' she said. 'Life's far more complex, usually.'

So nothing happened. The Royles and the Tanners got in touch with Mrs Stacey and said that they accepted there might be some blame on their side as well as on the Mason boy's, so they would not like to see him punished, especially. They pointed out that they had contacted Mrs Mason and suggested a hospital visit with some small gifts, but had been rebuffed rather rudely. They said, in any case, that as it was so near the end of term, Anna and David, and Rebekkah, would stay away for the rest of it, although they would 'almost certainly' return when the holiday was over.

Mrs Stacey, after a great deal of thought, wrote back to say she was confident that a 'minor incident' had been blown out of all proportion.

Louise Shaw did not see these letters, naturally, and in assembly, Mrs Stacey gave only a short and very general talk about 'the accident you will have heard about', which might have had an element of bullying in it – 'on all sides' – and which should be a lesson to them all, not least about the dangers of the chalkpit. The children were disappointed at the lack of blood and guts, Brian was infuriated by the head's hypocrisy, and Louise was surprised to find herself pretty well indifferent.

'What did you expect?' she asked him, in the pub that evening. 'She's decided it's too complicated to be solved. She did her best.'

129

'If that's her best, save us from her worst,' Brian snorted.

'What would you have done?' said Louise. 'Kicked them out? So that they could go and bully weaklings at another school? Kicked Simon out, so that he could go on being battered without you having to think about it? Given them all a hundred press-ups every morning? The truth is, it's a vicious circle. Simon's the sort of kid who's going to attract bullies wherever he goes, but it suits us to deny it. He's like your crippled goose, do you remember?'

'I remember very well. I remember that you denied it hotly. You disapproved of me for even thinking it.'

She nodded.

'I know. I hold my hands up, I admit it. The thing that horrifies me is that we're as bad. The kids pick up their attitudes from us, don't they? Which of the teachers cares for Simple Simon? Which of us actually likes him?'

'Simple Simon. You'd kill me if I called him that.'

'Exactly. I'm being honest, aren't I? How can we blame the kids for bullying when we feel just the same? It's horrible, Brian. I hate myself for even thinking it.'

There was a long pause. They touched their glasses, but they did not drink.

Then Brian said: 'So what's the answer? I'm only a humble PE teacher, but even I know we can't wring their necks. Is there an answer?'

She smiled briefly at his bitter little joke.

'Don't know,' she said. 'Eternal vigilance, certainly, but beyond that ... ? Trying to make everybody recognise that even kids like Simon have their worth? Trying to recognise it ourselves? We're all prejudiced, Brian. Mrs Stacey's prejudiced against a dirty shirt. Maybe we've got to examine our prejudices for what they are. Are you still awake?'

'I am,' he said. He laughed. 'But only just, joke-joke.' He laughed again, hopefully. 'It all makes my brain hurt. Film tonight? Later? You and me?'

'Okay,' said Louise Shaw.

Some days later, Anna and Rebekkah went back to the chalkpit, on a whim. They did not take David. Even as they walked down the access road they could see that something had been done. The notices were gleaming with fresh paint. **Keep Out**, they said, in black. And in shining red: **Extreme Danger**. Anna took hold of one of the gates and shook it.

'They've done a good job, haven't they? They've put new mesh in all the holes. I wonder if they've been along the fences, too.'

They looked all round them carefully before deciding to go in. All the other kids were at school and there were no adults in view. Rebekkah had been checking weak points.

'It's hopeless,' she said. 'They've done a really *terrific* job. I bet it would take ten minutes!'

'Two!' said Anna. 'Come on, race you!'

It took them five, and it was almost a dead heat.

After checking once more that they were entirely alone, they made their way to the pile of chalk and rubble at the bottom of the cliff, where Simon had come to earth. There were no other signs, no blood or anything.

'What do you think of it?' said Rebekkah, after a short while.

'What?'

'You know. What we did.'

There was a longer pause. It was a warm and sunny day, and seagulls were screeching high above their heads.

'We got off pretty lightly,' said Anna, in the end. 'Didn't we?'

Simon got bored in hospital pretty quickly, and hankered to get back to school. Being young, his wounds healed fast, and his memory of the avalanche, and his fear of being bullied at St Michael's, were soon forgotten. He had a plan to play on Miss Shaw's sympathy and get to be the monitor again. He guessed they'd buy another gerbil, if he pleaded hard enough.

Mrs Mason had nightmares about the chalkpit, and had vengeful, bitter thoughts about the Royle children, and Rebekkah, and their families. Simon didn't.

His one regret, really, was that he didn't have a friend to come and sign the plaster on his leg. But he had the nurses' signatures, and some teachers', and his mum's.

On the blank bits he signed 'Diggory' – many, many times. He liked that.

A PACK OF LIES
Geraldine McCaughrean

Ailsa doesn't usually pick up men in public libraries — but then M.C.C. Berkshire is rather out of the ordinary and has a certain irresistible charm. Once inside Ailsa and her mother's antiques shop, he also reveals an amazing talent for holding customers spellbound with his extravagant stories — and selling antiques into the bargain!

'Sparkling with wit and originality' – *Guardian*